Delight questions

"I do not agree with you [...]h pitching soiled straw fr[...]y uniforms or generals of nobility, but we have the cloak of truth."

"Truth is certain," Henry agreed, "but the cause takes time, effort—and the blood of men to lead it to victory."

Defiance etched her face. "Perhaps you do not truly harbor freedom and liberty in your soul."

"And perhaps ye do not really know me at all."

DIANN MILLS draws the broken to wholeness in her writing. She lives in Houston with her husband Dean. She wrote from the time she could hold a pencil, but not seriously until God made it clear that she should write for Him. After three years of serious writing, her first book *Rehoboth*, won favorite **Heartsong Presents** historical for 1998. In 2002, *Mail-Order Husband* won favorite **Heartsong Presents** historical, and she was voted a favorite author.

She is a founding board member of American Christian Romance Writers and a member of Inspirational Writers Alive. She speaks for various groups and conducts writing workshops.

DiAnn and her husband are members of Metropolitan Baptist Church, Houston, Texas, where they both serve in the choir, and she volunteers as a church librarian. Visit her Web site: *www.diannmills.com.*

Books by DiAnn Mills

HEARTSONG PRESENTS
HP291—Rehoboth
HP322—Country Charm
HP374—The Last Cotillion
HP394—Equestrian Charm
HP410—The Color of Love
HP441—Cassidy's Charm
HP450—Love in Pursuit
HP504—Mail-Order Husband

The Turncoat

DiAnn Mills

Heartsong Presents

A note from the author:
I love to hear from my readers! You may correspond with me by writing:

> **DiAnn Mills**
> **Author Relations**
> **PO Box 719**
> **Uhrichsville, OH 44683**

ISBN 1-58660-632-8

THE TURNCOAT

All Scripture quotations are taken from the King James Version of the Bible.

All of the characters and events in this book are fictitious. Any resemblance to actual persons, living or dead, or to actual events is purely coincidental.

prologue

1776

Henry O'Neill studied the blue waves slapping against the sides of the British war vessel as it sailed into Boston Harbor. He felt the wind gather momentum and the vessel sway from side to side. Glancing above the sails and tall masts to a gray, turbulent sky, he watched the clouds roll toward the bay. At least they would land soon on the American soil and be free of nature's pending fury. Henry believed in God, not omens; but a clear blue sky and a sparkling ray of sunlight flitting off the waters would have suited him much better.

Glancing down at his bright red jacket with its deep blue facing and white metal buttons, he could not help but feel proud of what his uniform represented. As a foot soldier in Colonel Hamilton's Twenty-first Regiment, he shared in the objective to help squelch the rebellion. These colonists were an unruly lot, but they were no match for King George's army.

No matter what lay ahead in the line of duty, serving the king provided the distinction of being a part of the world's strongest fighting force. The distinction also kept clothes on his back and food in his belly, although the latter hadn't settled well during the lengthy voyage. Henry cringed. He still tasted the nasty bile. His stomach had wretched more times than he cared to recall, and he could not wait to set foot on solid ground.

A twinge of excitement and fear raced up his spine. Henry never thought of himself as a hero; his livelihood before enlisting depended on weaving cloth, an honorable trade taught to him by his father. Unfortunately, his father couldn't feed all twelve of his brood in Ireland; and Henry had vowed not to go without food, clothing, and proper shelter again. This new land offered so many opportunities for a skilled craftsman, and he eagerly anticipated setting up his loom for business once he had fulfilled his responsibilities to His Majesty.

He stiffened. Yes, he'd fight for King George. Henry had declared his allegiance, his very life if necessary, to defend the crown and uphold the king's edicts.

A few short months should manage the rebellion quite nicely; then on to his new life.

one

January 1776

Delight Butler stuffed a folded piece of paper into her apron pocket and peered to the right and to the left of Boston's bricked street for any sign of redcoats. A gust of wind whipped around and caught her unaware, and she pulled her coat tighter to fight the biting chill. A few soldiers emerged from down the street and marched toward her and her sixteen-year-old sister, Charity. Although she believed they would not harm them, a measure of anxiety nipped at her heels nonetheless.

Where is he?

Sometimes she read the papers before delivering them to the designated patriot or member of the Continental army, but not today. William Taylor needed this as soon as possible.

"How much farther to the Taylor home?" Charity asked with a sigh. "Mama will be expecting us."

Delight frowned at her sister and adjusted the wooden bucket dangling from her arms. "Papa promised this to Mr. Taylor. We only have to cross over to Hanover Street."

Charity tossed her dark head, her mobcap trimmed in lace bobbing like a chicken pecking for grain. "I don't like walking with the redcoats marching by."

Delight stopped in the street, her attention focused on the approaching soldiers. Just the mere sight of them infuriated her, and the thought of flinging a jeer their way teased her mind.

"Sister?" Charity said impatiently with a stamp of her foot.

Delight found her senses. "We shan't be much longer, and I must say the walk home will be more pleasant without the sight of the British soldiers."

"I agree. I am simply thinking of the work awaiting us at home, and this cold has my fingers and toes numb."

7

Delight ignored her. She didn't have the time or the whim to indulge Charity. The soldiers moved closer; their hands gripped their muskets, poised and ready for a fight. Their boots pounded a rhythm against the packed snow, leaving the impression they stomped every patriot in Boston. A twinge of fear assaulted her, although not for her safety but for those defending freedom. She held her breath as they passed, not wanting to offer any respect for their pompous mannerisms, least of all for King George and his outrageous demands.

Will these despised soldiers ever leave Boston? "Let us hurry on," Delight said. She recoiled when the five soldiers turned onto Hanover Street. Suspicion crept over her. She picked up her pace in an effort to make Charity think she was obliging her.

"Has Mr. Taylor paid Papa for the buckets?" her sister asked breathlessly.

"He traded with Papa for an iron pot. We only need to make the delivery." How could she give him the document with Charity nailed to her side? She should have anticipated this problem when Mama suggested Charity accompany her and carry the second bucket for Mr. Taylor.

While they hastened their pace, Delight's gaze fixed on the soldiers who marched past Mr. Taylor's blacksmith shop. *Thank Thee, Lord.* She'd delivered more than one message to Mr. Taylor and knew his boldness. While soldiers waited for him to shoe their horses, they talked among themselves, and he forgot nary a word. Delight knew only one of his contacts, the man who'd given her the document today—a close friend of her father's who was a tanner by trade and lived on the outskirts of the city.

Once at the blacksmith, Delight peered into the darkness. "Mr. Taylor," she called out. "This is Delight and Charity Butler. We have come to deliver your two buckets."

The lean-looking man stepped out of the shadows and smiled broadly. "Good afternoon." He took the pieces and admired the craftsmanship. "What a fine job your father does, and I sorely needed these today."

"Papa will be pleased." Delight touched the crisp document in her pocket. Now, how would she be able to distract her sister?

"Do you have a favorite piece of Scripture?" Mr. Taylor asked.

Her code. If Charity had not been with her, she wouldn't have had to deal with procedures. Mr. Taylor needed to be assured of her purpose, and in the past she had been alone. "Yes, Sir, I most certainly do. It is from Psalm 37:4. 'Delight thyself also in the Lord; and he shall give thee the desires of thine heart.' "

"Ah, commendable. Your namesake verse, perhaps?"

We are using all our formalities today. I wonder why. "Yes, Sir. All of my sisters have one in accordance with their name."

"I've finished with the iron pot your mother requested. Would you like to take it with you?" Mr. Taylor gestured toward a bench in the corner, crowded with tools, nails, oxen- and horseshoes, and her mother's pot.

"Of course." Delight stepped over to retrieve the pot—a bit heavy, but she had Charity to help her carry it back. Spying a pile of nails, she elected to slip the message under them. Her fingers grasped the paper.

"William Taylor!" a man's voice boomed.

Charity gasped, and Delight whirled around to see British soldiers pointing their bayonets at the blacksmith. *Oh no. He has been found out.*

"That be my name," he replied without reservation.

Delight took her sister's arm and pulled her away from the soldiers' path. She could feel Charity trembling and feared the young woman might faint.

"The colonel would like to speak with you," the same soldier said. "He does not like to be kept waiting."

"About what matter?" Mr. Taylor crossed his arms over his chest.

"It matters naught to you. It is the king's business. Come along without another moment's delay."

Mr. Taylor laid his leather apron aside and glanced at

Delight. In the dim light she could not read his eyes, but the document still rested in her pocket. "Go ahead and take the pot—and give my utmost to Mistress Butler."

Delight nodded and lifted the pot from the bench. "Godspeed, Sir. Our prayers will be with you."

"He will need them," another soldier said with a chuckle.

❧

Elijah Butler pounded his fist onto the table, his round face and bald head flushed crimson. "How dare those lobsterbacks seize our friends and frighten my daughters! I wish I had the likes of King George for five minutes; I'd tell him to keep his soldiers out of our country!"

He plopped down onto his chair while Delight and her sisters set wooden bowls on the table for the evening meal. The tantalizing aroma of an oyster stew and hot bread with freshly churned butter filled the air. Once he had calmed and the family had taken seats on the benches, he thanked God for His bountiful blessings and asked Him to take care of William Taylor.

Delight lifted her gaze and glanced around the table at her mother and six sisters: Charity, Remember, Faith, Patience, Mercy, and Hope. *I am the oldest and expected to be a Christian example to my younger sisters. How would Mama and Papa feel about my assisting the patriot cause?*

The precious document in her pocket plagued her mind. She would have to leave in the dark of night in order to deliver it, and she hadn't the opportunity to read the contents or know where it should be delivered.

"I have made up my mind," Papa said firmly.

Stirred from her musings, Delight gave him her full attention. Papa never made rash decisions.

"We shall leave Boston. It is no longer safe for my family." He nodded at Mama with a slight smile. "We shall go to Chesterfield, where my brother tells me there is need for a cooper." He leaned in closer, peered from side to side, and whispered, "And if the British soldiers continue to disturb our lives, then I shall join the patriot army."

Mama drew in a sharp breath. "Praise God," she uttered, then moistened her lips. "Not that you might consider such foolishness as enlisting at your age, but that you have seen fit to rescue us from the yoke of the British soldiers."

Delight's heart pounded harder than Mr. Taylor's hammer against his anvil. *Chesterfield. How can I help the cause there? Who will be the courier here?* She looked at her father anxiously and asked, "How will we be able to leave?"

Papa nodded his understanding. "We cannot leave together, and it must be done in secrecy to avoid the soldiers."

Charity gasped at Papa's words. Because she was given to fainting, everyone looked expectantly at her pale face. "I'm fine, Papa."

He glanced at Mama. "You, Mercy, and Hope will leave tomorrow. I will give you detailed instructions later."

Delight picked at her stew. She was foolish to have her thoughts linger on her own importance. Of course the patriots would find someone else to deliver messages. Boston was full of those committed to the cause, those who longed to see liberty in the colonies. Indeed she thought too highly of herself. Perhaps she had fulfilled the destiny God intended, but she'd found meaning in her life by combining her faith in God with the efforts of the colonies to unite for freedom. Disappointment raged through her.

"Delight, have the happenings today stolen your appetite?" her mother asked. "Perhaps the soldiers frightened you more than you revealed to us."

"No, Mama. I am merely thinking." She wanted to voice her concern over the move but dare not sound disrespectful. "Papa, are you sure leaving our home is necessary? Can't we stay and be wary of the British?"

He shook his head. "I think not. When I look around the table, I see seven beautiful, brown-eyed daughters and their lovely mother. Our home is to be peaceful, not surrounded by strife and oppression. We will pack our belongings and sojourn to Chesterfield."

"When will all of us be together for the journey, Papa?"

Mercy, the eight year old, asked. Tears filled her eyes.

"Four days hence," Papa said and downed his buttermilk.

"We know you have friends here," Mama said gently. Even after seven children, her face bore few lines, and tenderness prevailed in her spirit. "But you will find new ones in Chesterfield."

Papa cleared his throat, an indication of the importance of his words. "Let us all be in constant prayer for a safe journey and a prosperous life in a new home."

"May we bring Bear?" Little Hope reached down to stroke the dog's sleek coat.

"Of course," Papa replied. "We shall try to take all we can. I have made arrangements with your uncle Matthew to secure us a good house and means for me to continue in building buckets and barrels once we arrive."

Delight's sisters chatted on. Some were excited and relieved; others were not. Luckily Papa was not of the mind that children should always be seen and not heard. He patiently answered their questions until all were satisfied.

But the discussion of the move only firmed Delight's resolve that at the first possible opportunity, she needed to read the document in her pocket and learn its destination. Only then could she consider what God intended by uprooting her world.

Long after the small house quieted and the only sounds were the even breathing of her family, Delight rose, dressed, and tiptoed to the fire, where the embers had not yet died. She carefully opened the document and squinted to read only enough to be able to determine that it should be delivered to the owner of one of the taverns near the wharf. Although the British had closed Boston's port, it was not safe for a young woman of eighteen to be about, especially after dark. Papa would be terribly angry if he discovered she was venturing toward such a rowdy place. But she must.

Oh, heavenly Father. Protect me this night from the dangers lurking where I must walk. Guide my feet, and shelter me in the shadow of Thy grace.

Somehow Delight found the courage to step out into the

dark with a lantern turned down low and hooded; but even so, she must not be seen—either by the town crier or by soldiers. She shivered in the frigid temperatures and stole toward the tavern, slipping on the ice and praying she didn't fall. Although she silenced her feet against the street, every sound alerted her to possible danger and reminded her of the vital information concealed in her right shoe.

She glanced up at a starless night hosted by only a quarter moon. How wonderful if God had blessed her with light. Her ponderings told her He had done so; she simply had to believe He honored her cause.

The time was long after midnight, and the tavern would be closed. Still, the area alarmed her. Every sound alerted her: the bark of a dog, the distant laughter, and the talk of soldiers. An eerie sensation trickled through her, as if someone trailed her steps. She had perceived this before and ignored it, but tonight the sensation felt so true. Nonsense, fear would not rule over her responsibilities.

When the establishment came in sight and the pronounced smell of fish met her nostrils, she didn't know whether to let out a sigh of relief or pray harder. To reach the back door of the tavern, she would have to risk attracting the attention of anyone who might be hiding in wait for a victim or wallowing in drunkenness. Worse yet, she might be detected by a redcoat. Chills raced up her arms, and she longed to turn and hurry home. Only her sense of mission enabled her to keep one foot in front of the other.

Delight realized she had held her breath until she felt faint. For the first time in her life, she wished she'd held the thoughts and desires of other young women her age—a home and family. Not that she didn't want those admirable blessings, but she felt duty-bound not to seek such a future until the war for independence had been won. Perhaps God had made a mistake, and she should have been born a man.

Clenching her fists, she rapped on the tavern's door lightly; the deafening sound caused her to hastily glance into the darkness. Along with the smells of the wharf, she inhaled the odor of sour ale. When no one appeared at the door, she knocked again a little louder.

"Who goes there?" a gruff voice called.

Delight took a deep breath. "One bearing Scripture fitting for the times to Cavin Sullivan."

The latch lifted with a squeak, and she stood before a man who in the shadows resembled a huge beast. "For all that is just and right," he whispered. In the next moment he grabbed her arm and flung her inside. "Lass, do you not know how dangerous it is to be out and about?" His stern voice, laced with a thick Irish accent, frightened her. In the darkness, this man could do anything.

"Are you not expecting something?" she asked. *Oh dear, I sound like an unscrupulous woman.*

He said nothing for several moments, but oh how conscious she was of this giant of a man. "Did you tell me you brought Scripture?"

"Yes, Sir." Her voice sounded shaky, not at all courageous. " 'Delight thyself also in the Lord—' "

"Aye, you've said enough," he whispered. "What bring ye?"

"Mr. Taylor was seized by the soldiers today."

"Indeed."

"I could not deliver my message, and I saw it goes to you."

She heard him expel a heavy breath.

"You are brave to risk the night for our cause," he said. "I expected a man."

She stiffened. "I am able to go undetected in most places." Delight reached down to unlace her shoe and to retrieve the document for Mr. Sullivan.

"Thank you, Lass," he whispered and took the folded paper. "Now, let me escort you home. It is not safe for you to be unescorted."

"I would be most obliged."

Suddenly his hand clamped over her mouth.

two

Terror reigned through Delight's body along with a measure of foolishness. She knew stealing out into the night to the wharf area without an escort invited peril.

Someone pounded on the door. "Open up. We are in need of spirits."

Mr. Sullivan moved not a muscle.

"Open up, or we will beat down the door. Our captain requests a bottle."

Redcoats! I've been followed. Caught!

Mr. Sullivan released her mouth and led her backwards. Surely all of Boston could hear her heart pound. "Just a minute. Can't a man sleep?" Mr. Sullivan called. He pushed her behind what she thought was a barrel.

"You can go back to bed once you have given us what we need."

The door creaked open. "And what would you like?" Mr. Sullivan asked.

"Rum!"

"And do you have payment?" Mr. Sullivan demanded.

A laugh rose from what must have been two, possibly three soldiers. "Talk to our captain in the morning. We were told to get a bottle of rum, that's all."

"Not without payment."

Silence invaded the room. *Please, give them what they want.*

"Either give it to us or we will take two bottles."

Loathsome redcoats.

"I'll get your rum," Mr. Sullivan shouted. Shortly thereafter the door closed. "Are you all right, Lass?" He bent to help her to her feet—this man whose face she had not yet viewed.

"I am well," she said softly.

"Come, this has been a hard night, and no doubt you seek

the comforts of your home." A candlelight's flicker opened the darkness, and she saw his face.

Once they silently disappeared into the streets, Delight gave thanks for her escort, and she prayed Papa had not detected her absence. Enough excitement had transpired for one day.

"I daresay this is the last time I can help," she said. Without waiting for him to question, she continued, "Papa is moving us to Chesterfield in three days. I fear I am of no service there."

"You have done more than your duty for the cause," he said seriously. "We are greatly indebted."

"I would like to continue, Sir. Please let those know who might need assistance in Chesterfield."

"I understand, and I will extend your concern."

When she saw the outline of her two-story home, she stopped. "I am quite safe now. Thank you for the escort."

"Good evening, and may your father's decision to leave Boston be a prosperous one."

Delight straightened her shoulders and moved toward the back of her home, for now she faced the ardent task of slipping inside without detection. In three days, all of this would be memories; but tonight, vivid sights and sounds raced across her heart. She longed to do so much more, but God obviously saw fit for her to cease in her work.

She held her breath and lifted the latch. Setting foot on the plank floor of her home somehow relieved the burden of the night's dangers. Only the stillness of sleeping inhabitants greeted her. *I thank Thee, Lord.*

Stealing up the stairs, Delight realized she would never forget the night's happenings. Weariness threatened to overtake her; even so, it would take a long time before her heart slowed its incessant pounding.

જાં

For more than sixteen months, Delight tried to appreciate the small town of Chesterfield, but it lacked the excitement of Boston. She'd hoped Papa would want to move back to their home city once the British deserted Boston in March of '76, but he elected to remain in the quieter town. News of the war trickled in, although the patriots of Chesterfield eagerly strove to fight for their beliefs. Tories disgusted her, for she felt their loyalty to Britain was out of fear. She refused to listen to their viewpoint and wished all of them would board the next ship back to England.

She listened and took note of a few patriots who held the qualities of leaders, all the while praying she could again be of assistance to the cause.

In the past, Papa had attempted to take the middle ground, as though they were Quakers who dared not take up arms. But even before they left Boston, she saw him lean heavily toward the patriot cause. The incident at Mr. Taylor's blacksmith shop was the turning point.

In Chesterfield, Papa often left the house in the evening and didn't return until quite late. Mama fretted constantly, and once Delight heard them arguing about the war efforts when he returned. She quickly assessed her father had joined the revolutionary cause and wanted to enlist in the Continental army. However, Mama stood her ground and insisted he remain in his trade.

"We have no sons, Elijah," Mama whispered through a ragged breath. "If we did, then one of them could take over the cooper business."

"Would you deny me the privilege of fighting for freedom?"

Silence permeated the house.

"My dear husband, I love you with all my heart. Is it so wrong for me to want you unharmed?" Mama's tears stabbed at Delight's heart. She understood her mother's sentiments and her father's longing.

"Freedom is always purchased with a price. I am not afraid to sacrifice my life so that our grandchildren will live without the tyranny of England."

"And deny our unborn child a father?"

Papa did not reply. The only sound came from Mama's muffled sobs. This baby was their eighth child, hopefully a boy for Papa.

Delight felt her own eyes sting. Frustration dug at her

senses. At least in Boston she could do her part, possibly enough for Papa's share. When the war for independence was won, she would tell him of the many times she had relayed messages to the patriots.

One of their new neighbors, Abby Rutherford, had brought a loaf of bread and a cheery welcome when they first arrived. She and her husband had two sons the ages of Mercy and Hope and seemed cordial enough until Mistress Rutherford mentioned her intense dislike of the patriots.

"We are of the mind that liberty is the utmost course for our country," Mama said pleasantly.

Mistress Rutherford stiffened and moved toward the door. "I am dismayed at how you feel about King George. He is our established king. I certainly hope you soon come to your senses."

Mama wiped her hands on her apron and stepped ahead of the woman to the door. "Thank you for the bread, Mrs. Rutherford. If you think a pompous, selfish man across the Atlantic cares about anything other than lacing his pockets with our money, then you have lost *your* senses."

Mrs. Rutherford stomped out, red-faced. Mama whirled around and faced her daughters. "We women may not carry muskets and bayonets, but we can surely sear the Tories' hearts with the truth. Remember, the truth shall set us free."

ə.

Henry fought loyally for the British. Not once did he regret his enlistment, knowing at the end of the rebellion, he would live out his days in the colonies. He spent the winter of 1776–77 in Canada, fighting bitter cold and hunger from rationed provisions. He didn't mind the vigorous training, for he acquired strength and a disciplined will about him. Pride and determination clothed him more securely than the white wool coat issued to keep him warm. He had made splendid friends. One in particular, Adam Bennett, had been drafted from a poverty-stricken area of London. In him, Henry found a kindred spirit.

On May 6, 1777, soon after the St. Lawrence River had

thawed enough to allow passage, General John Burgoyne arrived in Quebec. Pleased with the training of his regular troops, Burgoyne set June 13 as the date to launch a massive campaign designed to free New York and the surrounding areas from the patriots.

"I heard the captain talking last night," Adam said. He polished a black powder smudge from his musket before continuing. "Quite admirable of us, I might say. The captain said military brilliance had emerged from the Canadian forces."

"Aye, Adam. I'm pleased. What else did he say?"

Adam leaned closer, staring down his long, pointed nose. "General Burgoyne said with the British right wing division under Major General Phillips and the German left wing division under Major General Baron von Riedesel, we are indeed an impressive and disciplined force."

"I'm proud. This war will soon be ended, and we can all go about our business."

On June 13, twenty-eight ships and several bateaux headed across Lake Champlain toward Fort Ticonderoga, where the hastily retreated Continental forces gave the British success. The campaign continued, and Henry's optimism that the war would be quickly won gave way to endless fighting, following a long, grueling overland wilderness trail to Fort Edward. Henry faced fatigue and discontent in a land he had once believed was his destiny. He despised the rebel movement and vowed they all should be shot or hung for defying King George.

Just north of Albany, New York, at Stillwater, the fighting grew steadily worse. The Americans were proving to be a fighting force of their own.

Henry heard the order to advance. Gripping his musket, he charged forward amid the blinding smoke. The cries of wounded men and the blasts of gunfire spiraled terror through his body.

"Henry!" Adam shouted.

He turned to see his friend fall into bush and thorns. *Dear God, no!* Henry rushed to Adam's side and pulled him into a clearing. Blood gushed from his friend's chest and onto his uniform. Henry covered the wound with his hand, staring in horror at the crimson river flowing between his fingers.

"Let me bandage you." He looked for help, but his compatriots were involved in heavy fire. He saw another soldier fall.

"Spare yourself," Adam whispered. "Thank. . ." He breathed his last.

Henry held his friend a moment longer, not certain what he should do. The idea of abandoning Adam seemed cruel. Suddenly white-hot pain seared his upper leg. He grabbed the torn flesh and viewed the flow of blood oozing between his fingers. This time it belonged to him. A moan escaped his lips, and he fell beside the lifeless figure of his friend. Conscious of the battle going on around him, he continued to fire his weapon until blackness overtook him.

❧

August 1777

"I saw Connor Randolph staring at you after worship yesterday," Charity said with a smile. "He is quite handsome."

"He's a Tory," Delight replied. "I would rather cut off my right arm than look his way."

Charity's eyes widened, and the conversation seized the attention of Remember, Faith, and Patience.

"You should not say such things," sixteen-year-old Remember said. Known for her devotion to biblical teachings, most likely Remember would be reciting Scripture in the next breath. " 'But I say unto you which hear, Love your enemies, do good to them which hate you.' " She lowered her lashes in reverence.

Delight fought the anger rising inside her. Crossing her arms, she stiffened to do battle with her sister using a piece of Scripture from the Psalms. " 'I have pursued my enemies, and overtaken them; neither did I turn again till they were consumed. I have wounded them that they were not able to rise; they are fallen under my feet.' "

"How can you say such things when our Lord directed us to love our enemies?" Remember touched her heart.

"Watch me," Delight said. "I shall stitch those verses onto a sampler."

"Hush, you two," Charity said, her normally pale cheeks heightening in color.

Why did her sister even bother with peacemaking efforts? Delight wondered. After all, Charity had started the disagreement with her reference to a Tory casting his hideous glances Delight's way.

I must calm down. Considering her position in the family, Delight fought her desire to produce more rebuttals. "Forgive me for upsetting you. I simply have decided opinions about those loyal to England."

"I agree with her," Patience said, a rarity, given her timid nature. "Here in Chesterfield, our lives are quiet, but do you remember the soldiers in Boston? Have you forgotten how they arrested our friends?" She smoothed her apron, then toyed with a wayward strand of hair.

Wise thinking, Patience. Delight hugged her sister's shoulders. "Let's not quarrel, sisters. We have seen and heard enough about the war. We all want it to cease. For me, I cannot fathom an end until we are free of the British." When she saw the dismayed look on Remember's face, she touched her cheek. "You have heard Papa say he wants to fight. I know your heart."

Remember wiped a tear from her cheek and nodded.

The idea of Papa enlisting frightened them all, and Delight understood that each of her sisters responded differently.

"Quarreling will not make things better," Charity said softly.

"And I'm quick to argue and state how I feel," Delight said. "I am the oldest, and I need to set a better example."

"Is it so wrong to want everyone to live as Jesus wants?" Remember asked.

"No, not at all," Delight said. "Unfortunately, it is impossible when we are all so sinful. And what of us? We are a loving, Christian family, and we constantly quarrel with each other." Delight glanced into each sister's face and silently prayed. *Oh, Lord, please keep my family safe and help me to love them more.*

"I don't love the soldiers or the Tories," Patience said, her attention focused on the wooden floor of their home.

Charity reached for Remember's hand. "We will all try harder and pray more for each other and for the end of the war."

***

A week later, Delight still pondered that day's conversation with her sisters. She punched down the bread she was kneading, added more flour, and worked it into the dough. Baking bread had a way of diminishing her problems and unanswered questions—especially when she slapped the dough against the table.

Just this past Sunday, the minister at their meetinghouse had spoken against the patriots. He even held a special prayer service for those loyalist lads who had enlisted to fight with the British—the detestable Connor Randolph included. Papa, Uncle Matthew, and a few other men vehemently protested, stating the same should be done for those enlisting in the Continental army, but the minister refused.

"My household will no longer be associated with this meetinghouse," Papa announced, his voice booming above the mild-natured minister.

"My wife and I included." Uncle Matthew stood beside Papa.

"You are speaking against the king," Connor Randolph's father said. He rose to his feet and clutched the pew in front of him. "You and your patriot friends will be punished for your treason."

"Anyone who shares in our beliefs that freedom is worth any price is welcome." With those words, Papa nodded to Mama, and all of the Butlers left the building.

As Delight considered these events, she remembered her determination to love her family more and help keep them safe. Often she reasoned God had made a mistake by not making her a boy. She prayed for God to use her for His purposes, and she could not stop entreating Him to give the patriots victory and freedom for their land.

As she divided the bread dough and began shaping it into loaves, Mercy and Hope burst through the door with Bear right behind them. The two girls, ages nine and eight, were only thirteen months apart and looked very much alike, each with a splash of freckles across the nose.

"Where is Papa?" Hope asked breathlessly. "We have to tell him something important."

Delight smiled into their sweet faces. No doubt they had seen a snake or a fox while they took a break from their chores and rambled over the countryside. "He is due back any moment, girls. Can I help you with something?"

They both shook their heads and gulped for breath. For the first time, Delight saw alarm in their eyes and immediately feared the British had arrived in Chesterfield. "Why? What is wrong?"

Mama emerged from her chair at the spinning wheel. Delight read the silent concern in her face, too.

"British soldiers are just outside of town. They're marching this way," Mercy said between gasps.

Delight hid her dismay. *Is Chesterfield going to be another Boston? Are we to once more cower to the redcoats' demands?*

"But some of them look hurt," Mercy continued.

Wounded. Oh my, I didn't want Mercy and Hope to be exposed to the ugliness of war. Wanting to reassure the girls, Delight said, "I'm sure they are simply in a hurry to get somewhere. Would you like to help me with the bread?"

Before the girls had an opportunity to reply, Papa stepped inside. The two younger girls ran to each side of him.

"What goes on here, my angels?" Papa wrapped his arms around each girl.

"We saw British soldiers," Hope announced, "and we're frightened."

"There is nothing to be afraid of. Those soldiers are merely passing by. I witnessed them myself." Papa spoke in the gentle tone he reserved for the women in his household. "Do not concern yourself. Take Bear outside and engage him in a game of sorts."

"But what if they come here?" Mercy's eyes pooled with tears.

"If you see a soldier draw near to our home, Bear will surely alert me immediately."

Once the door closed and the two girls disappeared, he shook his fist and exclaimed, "Dirty redcoats, scaring my girls." He kissed Mama on her cheek and smiled at Delight, but his gestures did not disguise the anger on his face. "I will be about my business." He exited through the doorway, but not without Delight hearing him mumble beneath his breath. "I'm ready to use my musket."

Twenty minutes later, Bear began to bark. Mercy and Hope shouted for Papa. Delight opened the door to see a small band of soldiers moving their way. A wounded soldier was slung between two compatriots, his white breeches stained red with blood from a wound to his upper leg. Papa met them as they plodded toward the house. Mercy and Hope lingered behind, holding onto Bear.

"Absolutely not!" Papa said. "Take him elsewhere."

A soldier pointed his musket at Papa's chest. The little girls screamed, and Delight rushed outside with Mama right behind her. All of her sisters had gathered in the front yard, staring in horror at the scene unfolding before them.

"Calm your dog, or it will be a dead animal," the soldier ordered.

Papa narrowed his eyes. "Bear, quiet."

"General Burgoyne has issued an order! You, Elijah Butler, are to keep this soldier until he is well and we return for him."

"And if I refuse?" Papa asked boldly.

The soldier pricked the scarf tied about Papa's neck with his bayonet. "Would you like to face arrest?"

three

Delight stood speechless, understanding her father's proud stance in the face of the redcoats' demands.

"We will nurse him properly," Mama called breathlessly. She had grown so large with the baby, due any day, that she could scarcely walk.

Papa's gaze remained fixed on the soldier, and he ignored Mama. All the while, the bayonet rested within a hair span of his throat. "I have seven daughters and another child due any day. What do you expect from me?"

"You deal with his care," the soldier replied. "I have my orders from General Burgoyne. Take your complaints to him." He thrust a piece of paper into Papa's hands.

"We will find a place for him." Mama stepped to Papa's side and lifted a defiant chin.

"He can have my bed," Delight offered. Although it consisted of a small rope structure in a room shared with Charity and Remember, the bed could be moved into the hall downstairs, and she could make a pallet with her sisters.

The wounded soldier lifted his head, covered in a thick mass of auburn hair, most of which lay over his eyes. "Thank ye, Lass." His words were spoken in a thick Irish brogue. "I'll not be troublesome to ye."

He looked ghastly pale, and she might have felt some sympathy if he hadn't worn the despised uniform. Two soldiers half-carried, half-dragged him inside, where Mama directed them to the hall. They eased him to the floor, being careful not to further injure his leg.

"Has a doctor tended to him?" Mama peered into the wounded soldier's face.

"Briefly. Too many others needed the doctor's attention,"

said the soldier who had previously aimed his musket at Papa. "Fortunate for him, the doctor did not see fit to amputate his leg. See to it he does not grow worse." He gave Papa his attention. "Or it will not go well with you."

Lobsterback pig! Delight thought. *How dare you talk to my father this way? I wish I owned a musket; I really do.*

She studied her mother's face. Earlier today she had experienced pains, and now she had the enemy to nurse. When Mama attempted to bend to the soldier's side, Delight stopped her. "I will take care of him to my utmost. There's no need to make more work for you." She stole a glance at the soldier's bandaged leg, soaked in fresh blood.

"I can assist," Remember said. "I don't mind, really."

"I can manage," Delight insisted, promising herself that none of her sisters would be subjected to the atrocities of the British. "It shan't be toilsome to change the dressings." She reached for Remember's hand. "You can help me bring my bed downstairs."

"I will find some fresh bandages," Charity offered and disappeared with Faith behind her. Patience snatched up Mercy and Hope's hands and hurried toward the house.

A soldier who had helped carry the wounded man kneeled at his side. "We will be back for you soon, Henry. I'm sorry about all this—and Adam, too."

The man they called Henry nodded and closed his eyes, obviously in more agony than he cared to state.

Nearly an hour later, Delight dabbed at the soldier's brow. Huge droplets of sweat had beaded upon his face when he'd been lifted onto the bed. Once there, he fainted. She hated to admit that she had actually taken pleasure in his pain. Certainly God must be disappointed in her.

The time had come to change the man's bandage. She had a basin of water ready to cleanse the dried and fresh blood and a box of dried herbs that might be needed for a poultice. Not given to a squeamish stomach, Delight picked at the tear in the white breeches surrounding the wound to better examine the injury. As she pulled aside the bloodstained material, Charity, Remember, Faith, and Patience looked on.

"If you cannot watch this without becoming ill, I suggest you leave me be." She knew full well only Remember might remain—to pray for the man.

"You girls have chores," Mama said from the doorway. "If Delight needs assistance, she will summon you." She placed a mug of feverfew tea next to Delight.

Another concern crossed Delight's mind. "Is the baby coming today?" she asked, remembering the look of pain that had swept over her mother's face earlier when Papa spoke with the soldiers.

Mama nodded and offered an endearing smile. "I believe so. Please pray for a boy—more so a healthy, whole child. Your father would be so pleased if he had a son."

"Of course. And perhaps you need to be in bed?"

Her mother turned from the doorway and moved into the kitchen without a reply. She appeared to forget Delight had questioned her.

I know where I get my stubbornness. She focused her attention on Henry, who appeared to be studying her curiously.

He drew in a quick breath as she slowly unwrapped the blood-soaked bandage, which looked more like a shirt ripped into strips. "I be a thanking ye again for the care."

So the redcoat knows a few manners when it is imperative, Delight grudgingly acknowledged to herself. She looked at him and said pointedly, "I don't recall having much of a choice."

He said nothing in response, so she began washing the area around the open wound. A musket ball had grazed the leg deeply enough to cause a lot of bleeding, but he would recover as long as infection didn't set in. The flesh around it showed no signs of reddening, a good sign; yet a poultice of yarrow was in order.

"Aye, ye have a gentle touch," Henry managed to say through a ragged breath.

His comment amused her, especially when she could have been a sight more tender. "You will heal, if you take care."

"I will be talking to the Almighty about that. We've already held a few conversations." He dug his fingers into his palm; and for a brief moment, compassion seized her, but she refused to let that show. After all, Henry was the enemy.

"What is your last name?" she asked as she mixed the dried yarrow with some water and applied the herbal mixture to the wound.

"O'Neill. I'm from Ireland."

She smirked. "I can tell."

"But I intend to stay in the colonies after—"

"The patriots secure our freedom." She lifted a brow and met his attention without the least concern about hiding her agitation.

Henry scowled.

"We may not want the likes of those who contend with the king living here," she added.

"Your brashness might secure your family a wealth of trouble," Henry said.

She tightened the bandage around his upper leg a little rougher than necessary. Admirably, he did not complain or wince. "I daresay your wound may get infected, or you might eat something poisonous, or our dog might not like the way you converse with the members of this family and eat you."

He stiffened. "Aye, Woman, ye don't frighten me."

Delight gathered up the soiled bandages and dropped them into the basin. "I am not about to be threatened by a pompous redcoat. Go tell that to your General Burgoyne!"

ನಿ

If Henry had been able to stand, he would have dragged himself from the Butler household and reported the whole lot of them to his captain. But since he had no choice, he was forced to endure the insults aimed at King George. The thought made him feel even more furious—and helpless.

His leg felt like someone had touched him with a hot poker.

To be sure, the pain had not ceased for four days. At first he'd worried the doctor might amputate, then he'd worried infection might kill him. And now he had this! This insensitive rebel woman assigned to nurse him would rather see him dead.

He narrowed his eyes. Everything inside him wanted to explode, and she looked as though she felt the same. He'd met better company among Ireland's landowners than he now faced living with these disagreeable colonists. Delight was her name? Quite possibly the woman served as a handmaiden for the devil.

Taking a deep breath, he reached for the mug of tea while Delight swished her skirts and left the room.

Lord, help me with these dire circumstances. The rebels here in the colonies are most difficult. And I know the woman assigned to nurse me regrets her position. I am imploring Ye to heal me quickly so I can rejoin my regiment.

He lay back on the bed. War was not at all what he had expected. Men died, men were wounded, and friendships ended in a half breath; but he hadn't been prepared for the passionate loathing of so many Americans.

Henry persuaded his thoughts to turn to other matters, so he studied the neatly kept room. What few furnishings the Butlers owned were simple and plain. Two straight-back chairs rested against one wall with a spinet setting between, a deep wine-colored sofa against another, and a mirror hung to reflect the light from the fireplace and candles. A far wall held the portraits of Elijah Butler and his wife in their earlier years. He noted the kitchen was connected to the rest of the house, not like some he had seen where the cooking was done separately. He imagined the second story to be as neatly kept. This family did better than most.

Hours later in the twilight, he heard a commotion.

"I'm going after your aunt Anne," Elijah Butler said. "Delight, Charity, tend to your mother until I return."

Ah, the mistress is in her confinement. He slowly tried to raise himself, but he found no strength for the task. The sounds of excited female voices filled the house.

"Hush," Delight said. "Mama does not need us scurrying about like a bunch of chickens. Come, let's pray for her and the unborn babe."

Henry strained to hear the woman who had vexed him so. Could she be a follower of the Lord and Master, Jesus Christ?

"Heavenly Father, we are gathered here in concern over our mother and the unborn child. We are asking Thee to guard her and keep the babe safe in the shelter of Thy wings. Papa wants a son in a powerful way, so we're asking Thee to bless him with a boy."

"And mend the leg of the soldier we are keeping here," another voice added.

"That is very thoughtful of you, Remember," Delight said a moment later. "Lord, help me to hold my temper with him so I shan't disappoint Thee. In Jesus' name, amen."

Henry chuckled. Some aspects of this family were a bit amusing.

He slept fitfully during the evening. The events of the impending birth had the Butler family bustling about, and they seemed to forget him in the excitement, which suited him just fine. When darkness settled, Elijah entered the hall. He towered over Henry, the expanse of his shoulders outlined by the firelight from the kitchen.

"Mr. O'Neill," he said with a slight edge to his tone.

Henry ached from the day's journey and the endless pain in his leg. "Yes, Sir."

Elijah bent beside him. "Let me give you a word of warning. Are you a family man?"

"No, Sir. I have never married."

"My family means more to me than you could ever imagine. If I find out that you have harmed one of them in any way, I will cut your other leg off myself. My wife and daughters are the reason God gives me breath. They come second only to God, and my beloved country is third. For those considerations, I would gladly give my life."

Henry heard more passion in this man's words than from

many of his commanding officers. He didn't doubt for one minute that Elijah Butler would take an axe to his good leg if he upset his family. Visions of the man's daughters, especially Delight with her quick temper, raced across his mind. "I understand perfectly."

Elijah rose to stand over him again. His mood instantly brightened. "This is a fine night. A new birth is a blessing, and my sister-in-law says it shan't be too long." He turned and walked from the hall.

"Mr. Butler," Henry called out. "I will be praying for your wife and the babe. My mother birthed fifteen children, twelve living, and I well remember how we prayed for her."

The man spun around. "I've been lucky that all of my children have survived save a twin sister to young Mercy."

Henry watched the man disappear. Someday he wanted a wife and children, if God saw fit. And from what he had seen of the Butler family this day, they were a good Christian family, although he didn't know how they could reconcile their faith with their rebellion against the king.

Dozing off to sleep, he dreamed of his regiment and the constant drilling. Always the soldiers talked of breaking the will of the colonists who refused to obey King George. What did these people hope to gain by their rebellion? No finer life existed for those who fell under the jurisdiction of the crown. A twinge of something long-since past pierced his heart. He remembered the oppression of family and friends in Ireland, the starvation, and the endless work. He had elected to leave his homeland and make life better for himself. What price was freedom? For the first time, Henry wanted to know how these people viewed their circumstances—not that he intended to change his mind. After all, he'd made an allegiance to England, and he was an honorable man, willing to do whatever necessary in the service of His Majesty, noting Elijah had declared earlier the same about himself. Nothing more.

❧

Much later, Henry awoke to Elijah's shouts of, "It's a boy!"

Excited voices filled the house. "He is a fine-looking lad," Elijah continued. "Praise God."

"Oh, Papa, this is wonderful," Delight said.

"What is his name?" a much younger daughter questioned. "Will it be the same as yours?"

"Of course, my sweet Mercy. Elijah Paxton Butler."

The man's words tugged at Henry. How often had he heard the same gratitude to God expressed by his own father? These people were enemies, but they all prayed to the same God. The thought confused Henry to the point he could not go back to sleep. *If we all pray to the heavenly Father for protection and victory over our enemies, how does God decide who is the victor? Who is really on the side of God?*

❧

Delight's eyes burned from lack of sleep. She stirred eggs into the huge skillet, which had just held frying bacon. Biscuits baked, and the aroma teased her senses. How good they would taste with freshly churned butter and a generous helping of the berries Mercy and Hope had picked the day before.

For two nights, she had stayed up much later than her usual custom and talked with Papa, Charity, and Remember. Papa loved reminiscing about the birth of each of his children. But when the clock struck twelve, she and her sisters traversed to bed. Papa spent the remaining hours seated by Mama's bedside, holding little Elijah just as he'd done with her sisters.

The baby's birth had caused so much excitement in the Butler household. New friends in Chesterfield and Papa's brother, Matthew, and his wife, Anne, visited and brought their hearty congratulations along with a wooden rattle carved to look like a fish. Another neighbor brought a pudding cap for the baby, although it would be months before he would be toddling about and need the cap to cushion his fall.

The last time Delight had checked this morning, Papa had fallen asleep and Mama held the baby. What a true blessing for Mama and Papa. They loved their daughters and often exhibited a fierce protectiveness toward them, but now they had a dear son.

Delight felt a smile spread across her face and a few tears of joy sprinkle over her cheeks at the thought of little Elijah. She knew God had smiled on them despite the orders to house the redcoat.

Delight picked up the mug of chamomile tea she had brewed for Mama. The herbal liquid would help her get much-needed sleep. The other women in this family could take care of everything while Mama recuperated from childbirth. She smiled; they would all be fussing over who would hold Elijah.

Much to her distaste, she needed to check on Henry. Secretly, she'd named him the prisoner. His bandages should be changed again, and surely the man was hungry. Papa said it would take several weeks before his leg healed. Not a day too soon.

Midmorning, Delight heard the pleasant sounds of Mercy and Hope's laughter. They were nowhere to be seen, but she soon realized they were in the hall with the soldier. Angry that the girls had sought company with Henry, she stomped into the passageway, prepared to save her sisters from the enemy. Instead she found Mercy and Hope seated on the floor with their cornhusk dolls, conducting a tea party with the wounded soldier.

four

"What are you doing?" Delight stared in disbelief at her younger sisters' wide-eyed innocence.

Henry lifted a walnut hull in substitution for his intended teacup in a gesture to sip his pretend brew. "We are enjoying a spot of tea." His thick Irish tongue sounded humorous with his English statement, but she was in no mood to be jovial.

"Yes, Sister. We are also having our tea with sugar and cream and bread with apple butter." Hope lifted a piece of broken pottery that no doubt served as a saucer.

Mercy swiped a sprinkling of dirt from her indigo skirt and stared up with the gathered portion of her mobcap framing her face. "We're not doing anything wrong, Delight. Please do not be angry. Mr. O'Neill offered to play with us."

Delight crossed her arms over her chest and scrutinized the three before her. "You volunteered to play with two children?"

He offered a faint smile—the first she had seen or believed she would ever see cast in her direction by him. "Aye, the wee lasses were looking for a playmate; and since I am engaged in idle time and enduring the pain in my leg, well, I offered."

Since when do soldiers play with children? Suspicion inched through her thoughts. This must surely be a new ploy by the British, and Delight knew a devious act when she heard one.

"I'm the oldest of twelve back in Ireland," he continued. "Sometimes I miss me brothers and sisters." A rather sad look swept over his pale face and, as he peered out at her, through deep blue eyes.

Henry desired sympathy, but he would not get it from her.

34

Let him waste away his hours with children's games. She didn't care.

"Very well." She felt quite victorious in seeing through his words. She turned to leave, but another notion crossed her mind. "If you are going to have a tea party, why not the Boston Tea Party? Mercy and Hope could pretend to be the Sons of Liberty."

&

Henry dug his fingers into his palms. Oh, how Delight Butler vexed him. She twisted her remarks like a knife in a man's flesh. Why didn't she leave the affairs of war to men and the business of play to children? He found it no surprise that these rebels plagued the king. Anger brewed inside him and threatened to bubble over. If not for Mercy and Hope playing nearby and the threatening words of their father, he would lash out at this impertinent young woman without delay.

Instead he simply smiled and answered, "Thank ye for the suggestion, Miss Butler, but if we conducted that party, we'd have to dress as Indians and steal away in the dead of night like criminals."

Delight's face reddened, and her large brown eyes appeared to ignite like a raging fire. Clenching her fists, she swallowed hard, no doubt to maintain her composure in the presence of her younger sisters.

"Girls, I could use your help in preparing the noon meal." Delight smiled at her sisters.

How could one woman be so disagreeable in one breath and reflect an angel's smile in the next?

"Must we?" Hope offered a most dismal look.

"I believe so, but this afternoon you can visit Mama and the baby for a little while."

Mercy brightened and clapped her hands. "Dare we hold him?"

"It is quite possible." Delight bent to gather up a walnut cup and pottery saucer. "I believe there will be time today for us to have a tea party beneath the shade of the maple tree outside, with real milk and a biscuit."

"Will Mr. O'Neill join us?" Hope asked. "He is quite lonely, you know."

Delight tilted her head and touched the cheek of the youngest sister. "Oh, my sweet Hope, he cannot come outside until his leg heals."

"How sad." Hope rose to her feet and curtsied to him. "Perhaps another time. Thank you, Mr. O'Neill, for playing with us."

"Yes, indeed," Mercy echoed as she offered an identical curtsy.

"Thank ye for joining me, lasses. I appreciate your conversation." Henry did enjoy the little girls. Their delightful chatter eased the frustrations of war, the steady throbbing in his leg, and the memories of Adam's last moments.

Once alone in the hall, he felt his exhaustion, and the weakness embittered him. He clearly wanted to rejoin his regiment soon and put this captivity behind him. For a few hours he had indulged in children's play when in fact this was the home of the enemy.

A shadow grasped his attention. Delight stood in the doorway, carrying a huge knife and towering over him like an executioner.

Gracious, what is this woman intending to do now? Henry closed his eyes. "Miss Butler, did you have something to say?"

"You are to stay away from my sisters." Her voice stung with hatred.

"The young lasses sought me; I merely obliged." *I am not afraid of this woman,* he reminded himself. *Her father, perhaps, but not this snip of insolence.*

"I must ask you to discourage them in the future." She shook slightly.

"Is your weapon intended to add weight to your demands?" Henry had no regard for his safety at this point. With the burning agony in his leg, she could hasten his journey into the

Eternal, and he would not mind the least. "For it means nothing to me."

She stared at the blade and turned it over in her hands. "It would make a fine tool to amputate your leg, although I dare say the process might take a sight longer for me than it would a doctor."

He laughed and forced himself onto one elbow. "I do not frighten easily, Lass. I've experienced the horrors of war: the screams of the wounded, the sight of mangled bodies, and the death of a dear friend beside me. You are but a gray cloud in a vast storm."

Delight's face paled, and she clutched the knife against her body.

Immediately Henry regretted his bitter statement. "I did not intend to shock your sentiments, of which I ask your humble pardon."

She nodded, but for once no reply slipped from her lips. *She's a fair lass, too.* Henry noted the deep color of her pursed lips, the smoothness of her skin, and her wavy hair, the color reminding him of tea with cream.

"War is not a pleasant task, Miss Butler." Henry no longer felt compelled to punish Delight with words or jesting. Across his mind marched the memories of those he'd no longer see in this life. "Those whom we serve enlist us to do what they cannot comprehend alone. We train to kill, we march in honor, and we forget we are mortals who might not live to see the next sweet blue sky. For each battle, a certain number must die to attain victory, or we admit defeat."

She moistened her lips. "Nevertheless, it is a sad state of affairs, nothing to take lightly."

"Is your cause worth the deaths of good men like your father, who is celebrating the birth of his son?" Henry had not intended to sound morose. The words simply flowed from his heart, for he indeed ached with what he had seen and heard on the battlefront. He detested the rebels and the problems they caused in refusing to obey the king's and parliament's commands, but more so he hated the ravages of war.

Delight stared into his eyes. He saw her defiant stance coupled with determination, a look he'd quickly learned was a vital part of the young woman before him. "I believe, Mr. O'Neill, as my father says, freedom is worth any price. I only wish I could do more in the strife."

The incessant pain forced Henry to lie back. "What is this freedom you rebels seek to die for? Define it for me so that I might understand." He hoped she saw his seriousness. The matter had plagued him for months, especially since Adam's death.

Delight slowly anchored herself on the floor beside Henry. The faraway look and the moisture pooling in her eyes told him she believed wholeheartedly in the American cause.

"I would like to join this discussion." Elijah appeared in the hall with them. "If Delight does not mind." He sauntered into the hall and seated himself beside his daughter. Flashes of gray streaked through his hair, tied back with a piece of leather; and his eyes held the lines of age, but his body appeared lean and strong.

"I will tend to the noonday meal," Delight said, offering her father a smile.

"Your sisters are capable. I would prefer you remain with me. Your views are important, too." Elijah grasped his daughter's hand, his white blouson shirt brushing against her arm.

He truly loves his daughter, this man who more closely resembles their dog and yet exhibits the gentleness of a lamb, Henry thought. *What a strange fellow to value a woman's opinion. Is this another characteristic of the rebels?*

"Freedom is not a word to simply offer a definition, but a condition of the heart and mind so compelling it calls cowards to acts of heroism." Elijah spoke softly, reverently. "It is independence from oppression and a commitment to a way of life that knows no class or favoritism. It is a conviction of representation by all the people." He took a deep breath, his very countenance exhibiting pride. "A portion of the Declaration of

Independence says, 'We hold these truths to be self-evident, that all men are created equal, that they are endowed by their Creator with certain unalienable Rights, that among them are Life, Liberty, and the pursuit of Happiness.' "

Henry could not quarrel with the claim, but he wasn't certain about the contents. The words sounded more like a child's dream, and it troubled him. "What is this Declaration of Independence?"

"A document signed on July 2, 1776, in which the thirteen united American states declared their separation from England."

Which is why I am fighting this war, Henry thought. "Have you no loyalty to the king?"

"None, neither do I have respect. He brought this on himself when he taxed us unfairly in order to pay for his war with France. We were not even consulted before they demanded we pull from our pockets that which we have earned on our own."

Henry felt his temper mount. "But King George and the parliament have the right to exercise power."

"Why?" Delight did not raise her voice, but her chin quivered. "Does the king or the prime minister really care about you, Henry O'Neill, wounded in his service far from England?"

Henry swallowed hard. He had always been given to contemplation on serious matters before expressing his views. Elijah spoke of political affairs of which he had little knowledge, and Delight asked a question he could not answer. He recalled the poverty in Ireland and Adam's stories of the poor conditions in London. The aristocrats ruled over the impoverished. They had the financial means to educate their children and purchase land. Henry needed time to deliberate this strange way of thinking, for to him it sounded like a dream. And if he conceded to their way of thought, then Adam died for naught.

"A country cannot stand without those versed in authority ruling over the people," Henry finally stated.

Elijah offered a grim smile. "This United States of America will have all the people electing those of their choice to make laws and carry them through."

Frustration agitated Henry. "Your ideas are foolishness. England is the most powerful nation in the world—more than any rebel colonies—and they have the Germans and many tribes of Indians to assist them. You will lose and beg King George to draw you into his fold."

"Not I," Elijah said with quiet conviction. "I will die first for my God-given rights."

"And I shall pick up a musket and follow after you." Delight's tears trickled down her cheeks. Never had Henry seen such radiance

Have these people gone mad?

five

With her pale blue skirt wrapped around her ankles, Delight struggled to stand; but Papa lent a hand, righting her to her feet. He wrapped his arm around her waist and planted a light kiss on her forehead.

"Daughter, we need to pray again for this man's healing. Despite his beliefs being contrary to ours, he is loved by God, and we are wrong to hinder his healing by omitting prayers."

Oh, Papa, I know you are right, but this is so hard when I know he defies your very soul. Looking up at her father, Delight said, "Of course, shall I gather the others?"

He nodded, and she slipped into the kitchen to summon them. A few moments later, all seven sisters and their father held hands and bowed their heads around Henry. She glanced down at the soldier; curiosity etched his brow. He blinked, and for a brief moment she viewed a solitary tear.

"Almighty Father, we are heartily sorry for not beseeching Thee more often about the condition of Henry O'Neill's leg." Papa's voice, his prayerful tone, thundered about the hall. "We implore Thee to heal him and make him whole again. We also ask that Thou wilt heal the differences between us. Show the errant their sins and increase Thy glory. In the midst of war, we forget Thy bounteous love knows no manner of men. May the world see the victory of liberty comes from Thee. In Thy Son's precious and holy name, amen."

For the first time, Delight felt the nudging of her heavenly Father to treat Henry with love. But her heart refused to sway. *Father God, I am so confused. Help me, above all things, to be a godly woman convinced of my purpose in Thee.*

During the following week, Delight chose to have a sister accompany her when she tended to Henry and prompted others to serve him his meals. The mere notion of being alone with him tugged at her conscience. She felt a peculiar mixture of anger and guilt in the presence of this man whom she wanted to hate but knew she should not.

"Your leg is healing properly," she said one morning while placing a clean bandage over the wound. Patience sat by her side, gathering up the soiled rags to wash.

Henry offered a faint smile. "Splendid. May I trouble ye to ask how much longer it will be before I am healed?"

Delight shrugged. "I daresay not as quickly as you might fancy. In a few days, you might try to stand, but even then it will be days before you can walk unassisted—or join your regiment."

"Aye, and I remember a few days ago when sitting up was an accomplishment." He released a sigh. "This wasting away of hours plagues my mind. If only I could toil at something."

"Soldiers are required to stay on their feet," she replied, not at all condemning, but truthful. "What can you do?"

"I'd settle to be working at my craft."

She lifted her gaze to meet his. *He does have kind eyes.* "And what is your craft?"

"I weave cloth, taught to me by my father."

"An honorable trade." Delight secured the bandage in place. No longer did she take comfort in his pain.

"I'm proud of my skill. I wanted to come to the colonies and set up my loom."

Understanding nestled into Delight's mind. "So you joined the British army?"

Henry nodded. " 'Twas the only way I could afford passage. Life in Ireland is quite difficult."

"So now you make life hard for us? If you want an easier way of life with more opportunities, then you are fighting for the wrong side."

Henry shifted. "I know you are convinced of my error, but I must be loyal to my king."

"Again, I ask why."

Henry said nothing, and Delight did not feel compelled to taunt him further with her convictions. He leaned back onto the pillow and clasped his hands behind his head. "I need to ask your father about the affairs of the war."

"Shall I fetch him?" Patience asked.

"That is not necessary," Henry replied. "I shall inquire of him later."

Delight deliberated revealing what she knew. What harm would it do? She realized no good would come from her boasting and purposely spoke softly. "I hear your General Burgoyne is not faring well along the Hudson River."

Henry closed his eyes. "Would you mock my loyalties, Lass?"

"Indeed not. I speak the truth clearly."

He moistened his lips. "What do you know?"

"At a place called Freeman's Farm on 19 September, a fierce battle took place in the afternoon." She paused. A wave of guilt swept over her at relaying the information.

"What else happened?"

She took a deep breath, realizing God did not relish any man losing his life. "Nearly six hundred of General Burgoyne's men were killed, wounded, or taken prisoner."

"So he surrendered?"

"No," she said sadly. "Americans withdrew at nightfall, but they did not have the casualties of the British. I expect there will be more fighting shortly."

A wave of sadness appeared to beset him by the way he sighed heavily and cast his gaze away from her. Delight knew not how to continue the conversation. "Come along, Patience. We are finished here."

"Thank ye, kindly," he said, obviously distracted.

Delight gathered up the basin. *My heart is softening toward Henry. How extraordinary. I might not have been so eager to report the conditions of war if the British had not lost so many men.*

≈

Late into the night of the third week of Henry's recovery, he lay awake while a hundred thoughts raced about in his head. Tonight, he had prayed until no more words would come. He felt dirty, a traitor to the king for the substance of his musings; but he could not rid himself of the rebels' beliefs.

I would be hanged or shot for these treasonous ideals. Still his mind continued to wander. He'd viewed enough of the Butler family to see and feel their passion for freedom. Henry shuddered. Had he no respect for Adam's death and the countless others who had fallen by the Americans' hands? Rather he had died than face this disillusion about himself.

All the talk of liberty had soured his mind to those values deemed important by the British. Yet a haunting recollection and a poignant memory of his life in Ireland nibbled at his soul. Hungry brothers and sisters, mounting taxes, no hope for a future with the rule of landowners—all these things seared his heart. If Ireland had been in revolt, he would have picked up a hoe or a stick for his homeland.

I know how these rebels feel; but in understanding them, do I dare side with their cause? If he confessed his true feelings, he admitted a kinship to them.

Shortly after Henry had succumbed to rest, he awoke to the low hum of voices. He recognized they belonged to Elijah, his wife, and Delight. Darkness prevailed except for the faint light of a candle, and he focused his attention on every word.

"Elijah, cannot someone else deliver this message?" Mistress Butler wept with her soft request.

"There is more fighting along the Hudson. Our troops need the information. I have no choice, my dear Elizabeth. My conscience gives me no rest."

"But the danger," his wife continued, "and you wish to take Delight?"

"No one will suspect a man and his daughter delivering goods. We shan't go far, and danger will be beyond us. Once I make the delivery, I will be home immediately."

"Mama, please understand. I want to go and help Papa. God will be with us; He will be our shield and protector."

Delight's voice rang out true as always. If the young woman had any doubts about the dangers and risks of this rebellion, Henry had never heard them.

"What if soldiers arrive to question Henry? Most assuredly he has heard every word. What will become of us?" Mistress Butler reasoned.

Elijah drew in a heavy breath. "I believe he will honor our home. He is a God-fearing man, one who knows the way of the righteous. He wears a British uniform, but his heart strengthens to our cause."

Silence echoed around them. "Very well," Mistress Butler whispered. "Godspeed. I'll prepare a bundle of food while you hitch up the wagon and ready yourselves. How long will you be gone?"

Again no one spoke. Elijah must have motioned to his wife. "If all goes well," he said, "we will be spending the evenings in various homes along the way."

"Am I to suppose you have other duties along the way?"

Elijah's boots clopped across the floor. "Yes, my dear. Not a moment shall be wasted."

All of Henry's earlier thoughts resurfaced. A bit of relief washed over him in not knowing their destination. He felt no ill toward Elijah and his mission. Quite the contrary, he rather envied and admired their courage. *Oh, Lord, I cannot fathom having such faith in one's convictions. I am greatly troubled. In my pledge to serve the king, I should turn Elijah in. Even while I pray, my heart is twisted and turned in searching for the truth. But he is right. I could never report his workings to the British.*

❧

In the dark of early morning with only the stars and a three-quarter moon lighting a white path, Delight rode with Papa in silence. They traveled along a solitary path toward the rendezvous point in New York with the rhythmic sound of the horses' hooves easing her mind like a lullaby. Tucked away in her left shoe was the precious information for General Gates.

The warm evening and the lull of the wagon made for her half-awake, half-asleep state.

"Would you like to lie down in the wagon?" Papa's question broke the silence.

"I think not. I like riding here next to you."

"As though you were a little girl again?"

Delight smiled and linked her arm into his. "You have always been tree height to me, Papa."

"Someday, probably sooner than I desire, another man will inspire you to those sentiments."

She laughed lightly. "He'd have to possess all of your fine attributes."

"All?" he teased. "Shall the poor man also have my faults?"

"Oh, Papa, you have so few."

He roared, sending his mirth out into the night. "I believe you need to have this discussion with your mother. She might enlighten you."

Delight leaned on his strong shoulder. "You are going to enlist, aren't you?" She whispered the words as though Mama rode with them.

"I am anxious to do my share."

"Is that your second mission in New York?"

"Possibly."

"But you are contributing to the cause now."

He paused before continuing. "This is not the first time."

Guilt crept through her about not telling Papa what she had done when the redcoats occupied Boston. "Is it not enough?"

"Not when it plagues a man's heart and mind to do nothing less for the freedom of his family."

Tears stung her eyes. "You should be an orator."

"A cooper suits me fine."

"A man should always seek higher aspirations," Delight insisted.

"I am, Daughter. It is my fondest wish for my children and grandchildren to proudly state their father and grandfather fought in the war for independence."

"But—"

"Not simply in the capacity of carrying information."

Delight felt a yoke of sadness. "I understand, for as a woman I have wanted to do so much more."

"Your mother and Aunt Anne are planning to melt down pewter next week and make musket cartridges."

"And I will help."

Papa hurried the pace on the horses. "Your soldier must not discover this."

"Who? Certainly you don't mean Henry. I would never reveal patriot information."

"Your sisters might speak unawares; that is why your time with Mama and Aunt Anne must be in secret."

She nodded and closed her eyes, more weary than she'd originally believed.

"Henry is a good man," Papa remarked. "Our plight for freedom is not unknown to him."

Irritation clouded over her. "What do you mean?"

"Delight, remember how Henry told you he joined the British army for transportation here from Ireland? For a better way of life?"

"And he is a weaver of cloth by trade."

"Do you not see? Henry is no different than my father coming to America to establish his cooper trade or the thousands of others who braved the dangers of ocean travel to better themselves and their families."

Papa's words made sense; and although Delight distrusted Henry, he often displayed a likeable side. "I comprehend what you are saying, but how do you propose to convince him?"

"Through prayer and what he senses in our family. The longer he lives in our home, the longer he sees our passion for liberty."

She sighed. "One afternoon Mercy and Hope were playing with their dolls in the hall. When I listened to their chatter, they were imitating you and Mother discussing your enlistment."

Elijah chuckled. "And what was the result?"

"With the girls, Mercy enlisted despite Hope's protests. Of course, Henry heard every word. At the time I merely found it all humorous; but his privy to the game is, as you say, an influence to our way of thinking."

"And you, Delight, are the biggest influence in his life."

"Papa, I'm afraid you are sadly mistaken. Neither of us is prone to pleasantries. We barely tolerate each other."

"Do you know why?"

She righted herself from his shoulder. "I have no notion whatsoever other than I have tended to him while he recovers."

"Ponder on this matter. You are a loyal patriot and a godly woman. Of late, I have noticed you are kinder to him, but you have not relinquished one bit from our cause."

And I shall not deviate. "You would like for me to be gentle, but firm?"

He turned and smiled broadly. "A wise and beautiful daughter I have."

"For you, Papa, I can do what you ask. Sometimes he is not entirely intolerable."

Elijah's laughter rang around them. "Delight, I do believe the two of you would make a fine pair—providing he forsook his redcoat ways."

Delight bit back the remark she'd have eagerly passed to her sisters if they had mentioned such a ridiculous notion. "Papa, surely you don't mean such?"

"Indeed, I do. I see the way the man looks at you and is thoroughly confused, and I see the way you are vexed with him."

"That is not an indication of love."

"Is it not? Perhaps this is another matter to discuss with your mother."

Out of respect, Delight chose not to reply. Never in a hundred years would she consider Henry O'Neill a proper suitor—not even if he enlisted in the Continental army and became a general overnight.

six

Much to Henry's confusion, he sorely missed Delight. Her wit and clever mannerisms kept his mind occupied, although he could live without the sarcasm. She made him feel alive. By their battling of words over the war, he could once again imagine carrying his musket and exchanging conversation with his compatriots. Never, in all his days, did he think he would miss a lively discussion with an argumentative woman.

In moments like these, he recalled his time with Adam. His friend had said he'd been drafted into the British army along with many young men of poor means. Henry pushed Adam's memory aside. Neither unshed tears nor bitterness would bring back his friend. More so than ever, Henry felt guilt pricking him like a burr, for his sentiments leaned toward the rebels. He agreed with most of their complaints.

Eager to depart from this room he had come to regard as a prison, Henry inquired of Charity for a fallen limb. She and Faith secured one, and with a little effort, he trimmed and fashioned it into a crutch. His restless spirit yearned to be outside even if it meant more pain. The weather had grown slightly cooler, and he longed to linger on a grass blanket with Bear and enjoy the first whispers of autumn.

One aspect of his confinement embarrassed him. He earnestly desired the necessary room rather than have to endure one more day with the chamber pot. He cringed each time Delight lugged it from the room—and she was always quick to note her disgust. For that concession alone, he'd crawl from the Butler home. Once he secured his freedom, he would beg Mistress Butler for a set of Elijah's clothes while he mended the huge tear in his uniform breeches.

When Henry was ready to try out his crutch, Charity,

Remember, Faith, and Patience offered aid; but he stubbornly refused their assistance and struggled to his feet. *Wish they would go about their business. This is difficult enough without women hovering over me.* Forcing his weight onto his hands, he leaned on his good leg and pulled himself up far enough so that he could grab the crutch. He sweated profusely but dared not give in to the pain. Once he steadied himself, he glanced into the anxious sisters' faces and grinned.

"Look here, Lasses. I am ready for a race." He moved about the hall until he mastered the technique, then set his sights on the kitchen. From there he'd venture into the blessed outdoors.

As he hobbled across the wooden floor, he could hear the birds and smell something pleasant, which was a sight better than himself. Bear walked alongside him, seemingly offering encouragement. Odd, the dog had become a constant companion after Delight declared the beast might eat him. He stopped to take a long look at the kitchen—the source of laughter, tantalizing fragrances, and more than one quarrel among the sisters. From this room came a world he had grown to admire and respect. During his initial entry into the home, his suffering had blinded him to almost everything. But now, spotless best described the Butler's kitchen, with rising bread—another pleasant smell—and the tart sweetness of a bowl of apples. He'd forgotten how wonderful life could be. Henry vowed to always treasure his two legs and the freedom to have them take him places.

Thank Thee, Lord.

Outside in the bright sunlight in the company of the young misses, he trudged toward a maple tree. Already he required a rest but felt too proud to confess his weakness. "I should like to sit in the shade of this glorious tree and enjoy a most beautiful day."

Henry's gaze drank in the beauty of changing leaves in gold and scarlet. The air was cooler, too, refreshing. How much he had missed in a few short weeks.

"Would you like something to read?" Remember folded her

hands primly in front of her. At times he wanted to laugh at her pious habits, for most surely her sisters mocked her mercilessly. Yet Miss Remember beset him with her servant's heart. Aye, he should follow her example.

"A Bible would be fittin' and anything else ye might have." He dropped the crutch and eased onto the soft ground, relishing every blade of grass beneath him. He tugged at one and held it up to the sunlight splaying through the tree branches, examining every strand. "I believe I've found heaven," he announced to the young women surrounding him. Glancing about, he wondered where Mercy and Hope had gone. "The little lasses, are they not out and about?"

"They're with Aunt Anne," Charity said. "She has a little boy their age, and the three play together famously."

He nodded. "Children need those times before they spend their lives working." He recalled well the day when whimsical inspirations were put aside to help provide for his brothers and sisters.

Once Remember returned with a Bible and an additional book, the sisters left him alone to read. Bear curled up next to his side and laid his mammoth head on Henry's lap. He breathed in the wondrous earth. Always given to the spaciousness of God's creation and a driving need to be outside, the three weeks of recuperation had deprived his natural instincts. Even when weaving in Ireland, he had the loom beyond the confines of four walls, surrendering only when night fell or the elements of weather prohibited his craft. That is why he enjoyed the rigorous training of the army while others complained.

Henry grasped the book Remember had brought to him. He curiously read the title: *Common Sense* by Thomas Paine. How peculiar, he hadn't heard of this title before. Perhaps the reading would spin away his hours. Completely immersed in the curious topic, he read for the next hour. One portion in particular, in which the writer addressed the purpose of kings, resonated with him.

Paine wrote, "Government by kings was first introduced into the world by the Heathens, from whom the children of Israel copied the custom. It was the most prosperous invention the Devil ever set on foot for the promotion of idolatry. The Heathens paid divine honors to their deceased kings, and the Christian world hath improved on the plan by doing the same to their living ones. How impious is the title of sacred majesty applied to a worm, who in the midst of his splendor is crumbling into dust."

Had Mr. Paine written the truth or merely twisted it to suit his own purpose? Henry felt the conviction of the man's words sear his heart. God be his judge, every word of *Common Sense* spoke to the core of his being.

❧

Near dusk on the third day of their travels, a few miles inside New York, a man on horseback approached Delight and her father.

"Are you a stranger to this fair country?" The rider reined his stallion in close to the wagon. The horse was a fine one indeed, its coat a silky black; and it pawed at the ground, indicating a desire to run with the wind. The animal's master offered an incredible smile, sinking deep dimples into the corners of his cheeks.

"A sojourner, my friend." Papa brought the horses to a halt.

An odd reply for Papa unless. . .

"Ah, we are all but travelers on this earth for as long as the Lord blesses us," the young man replied. "Pray tell, where are you bound?"

"Where the soil breathes of liberty."

The young man smiled. "I'm honored to meet you, Sir. I've heard courageous tales about your endeavors."

I was correct in my assumption. Pride soared through Delight at Papa's valiant stand for the patriots.

Her father reached out to shake the man's hand, then nodded at Delight. "This is my daughter."

The young man extended his hand to her. "A pleasure to

meet you, Miss. I shall be near your home two weeks hence, the Lord providing."

"Do honor us with your presence," Papa said.

"Thank you. I shall most certainly do so." He tipped his tricorn hat.

"We look forward to seeing you again," Delight added. She felt a glimmer of warmth spread over her cheeks at his engaging smile. She must ask Papa his name, since they had not been properly introduced.

"Pardon my hasty departure, but I must be on my way," the young man said.

"Of course." Papa turned to her. "Your shoe."

She hurriedly removed it and produced the document for her father. In the next instant, the young man turned his steed and disappeared into the brush. A strange sensation flashed through her body.

"And who might that be?" Delight's cheeks grew hot at the realization of her interest in the dark-haired young man with the dimpled smile, and she hid her confusion by bending down to put on her shoe.

"James Daniels, the son of an influential patriot. Both have worked closely with Sam Adams and the Sons of Liberty," Papa said, picking up the reins. "He's not married."

Delight caught her breath. "I simply wondered what his name was." *First Papa mentioned the most absurd possibility with Henry, and now he indicates Mr. Daniels is not married. Is he anxious to marry me off?*

"I merely mention his marital status because he works diligently for the patriots, often transporting information through enemy lines. He's been beaten by loyalists, wounded by British soldiers, has witnessed his father's death at Bunker Hill, and watched while his home burned to the ground, yet still he refuses to settle for anything less than liberty."

Delight's heart pounded hard against her chest. Such valor! Such heroism! That was the sort of man she wanted to share a home with one day, not the likes of a redcoat named Henry

O'Neill with his carrot-top hair and unbridled loyalty to the British.

The matter of Henry had better be laid to rest. She had given Papa her word to treat him as a friend and a guest in order for his Tory heart to soften, but nothing else. And what did Papa mean by referring to Henry: "I see the way the man looks at you and is thoroughly confused"? No mind, she didn't intend to explore it another minute. The thought repulsed her.

That night, Papa and Delight slept under the wagon. They were anxious to return home and had traversed long into the evening until exhaustion prevailed against them. Even then, Delight's mind reeled with the happenings of this cherished time with Papa. She'd witnessed a side of him that brought tears to her eyes—a true patriot. One day, she would draw her children to her side and tell them about their grandfather. Sooner than those days, she'd reveal her own small part in the war, although she still desired to do more than make musket shells.

James Daniels existed as another matter: quite handsome, that man. His smile could charm the bark off a tree. In short, she wouldn't mind his visit at all.

Two days later they finally made it back to Chesterfield. The small village had become home, but Delight sorely missed the excitement of Boston. Mercy and Hope met them with enthusiastic affection as though they had been gone for months. Mama and the rest of Delight's sisters filed out one by one to offer their hearty welcome and share in Papa and Delight's embraces.

"Did you have a pleasant journey?" Mama eyed him suspiciously. She knew Papa's designs.

He lifted baby Elijah from her arms and held him close. "Tremendous success, my sweet Elizabeth. I will share it all with you after dinner tonight." He sniffed the air. "Do I smell venison stew? All the while we were gone, I pondered your fine cooking. Nothing compares to it."

Mama shook her finger at him; her large, brown eyes twinkled, giving away her feigned irritation. "Elijah Abraham

Butler, you most assuredly have done something of which I shall disapprove. Is that where your compliments lie?"

Papa graced her cheek with a kiss. "And how is Henry faring?"

She released a sigh, then laughed before throwing her arms around his neck. "He is doing quite well." She pointed to the maple tree where Henry waved. "He has set up a loom and is weaving all sorts of marvelous things."

So now he captivates the heart of my mother? Delight could scarce believe her ears.

Charity nearly bubbled with excitement. "Come see, Papa. He has begun weaving diapers for Elijah."

"And he is able to weave black-gauze aprons, damask cloths, and a host of other wonderful things," Patience added.

"Wonderful!" Papa strode toward the maple tree, carrying Elijah, while Mercy and Hope nestled close to their father's side. "Greetings, Henry."

"Aye, Elijah. We missed ye." Henry grinned. "And ye, too, Delight."

I fail to believe you missed me. She released a heavy sigh. His comment irritated her, since they rarely enjoyed each other's company.

"I have taken to repay ye for your kindness," Henry continued. "Mistress Butler states some of my goods are not available here."

"True," Papa replied. "We have need of your fine services." He examined Henry's work and complimented his craftsmanship. "I'd like to keep you employed. The entire town could use your services."

"The British army would not agree with you, Sir." Henry's blue eyes fairly danced; a smile twisted at the corners of his mouth. Never had he talked so freely and acted so lively.

"We might be able to arrange something."

Papa, this daring invites trouble. You cannot trust the enemy.

Henry chuckled. "I do long for this war to be abated, for I

miss my trade." He peered around Papa to where Delight stood. "See, your generous care has given me strength to spend me days outside."

"I see that," Delight said. The smile he offered made her uncomfortable. A vision of the helpless, wounded soldier who relied on her assistance strolled through her mind. Why did she suddenly prefer the hurting man to the one on his way to wholeness? Confusion needled at her. She disliked the man immensely; and once his leg healed, he would be gone. That thought should give her tremendous pleasure. But it didn't, and an inkling of validity in her father's words made her furious.

"Soon I will be running like a strapping lad," Henry said. "Already I'm leaning less and less on the crutch."

"In your haste, are you causing more harm to your leg?" Delight instantly regretted her question. She wished Papa had never indicated his observations about Henry.

Henry's gaze met hers, causing another flush of warmth to her cheeks. "Me thinks the use makes me stronger, but I thank ye for the concern."

She felt the stares of her sisters like a sharp sword. No doubt, they would have thought little if she had returned his comments with a sharp retort. "I. . .I hope you understand your healing is of utmost importance to all of us."

"Come along." Papa's voice rang out above the silence. "I am famished, and I'm sure Delight is as well."

"Shall we call you when the meal is ready?" Mama asked Henry. "Or do you wish to join us now?"

"This is your family's time together," Henry replied, already scrutinizing his weaving. "There is still more than an hour of daylight left, and I am eager to complete this piece. In fact, I should most enjoy eating here."

"Very well." Mama linked her arm into Papa's. "I will have one of the girls bring you a generous portion of venison stew."

"Please, Ma'am, could Miss Delight bring it to me?"

seven

If Delight had set her mind to behave like a heathen, she'd been given the opportunity. Her first evening at home, and Henry wanted her to deliver his meal? If he could hobble about on his crutch, he could make his way to the kitchen when he finished his weaving.

As they strode toward the house, Papa stepped to her side and whispered, "Remember our conversation? This is an opportunity for you to extend Christian love and further instruct him in the way of patriots."

She obediently nodded but inwardly cringed. "Yes, Papa."

"When darkness settles, I'll invite him to a game of checkers and afterward chess. I feel merriment in my bones."

Delight knew the details of Papa's evening plans skirted around the war. He merely wished to postpone telling Mama he had enlisted in the Continental army. He had money stored away if times got lean before his return, and Uncle Matthew and Aunt Anne had already shared an abundance of vegetables and apples. All of the girls had been busy helping Mama preserve food for winter, from dried beans and squash to fruit preserves. Soon they would be cooking thick, dark apple butter flavored with sugar and cinnamon and pouring it into jars. Aunt Anne had given them rhubarb sauce from the spring and jelly from wild berries. Before Papa planned to leave, he'd help Uncle Matthew butcher pigs, sheep, and cows for the long winter ahead. Already, hams hung in the smokehouse.

Enduring cold weather without Papa sounded more dismal than the inches of snow that would drift against the sides of their house. At least they had the companionship of Uncle Matthew and Aunt Anne—and there were other dear folk in Chesterfield, too—but how she longed to return to Boston.

Delight shook her head. Dwelling on her gloomy situation would not change the current circumstances.

Casting aside her contemplations, Delight took a pottery plate of the thick stew, a chunk of bread, and a pewter mug of milk to Henry. His request still irked her. Since when did she become his keeper?

Remember your word to Papa. He sees a patriot's spirit in the man, whether you do or not.

Henry obviously didn't see her approaching, for he stirred not a muscle while he attended the loom. His breeches had been mended in her absence, albeit the stitching looked a little less than even, but it did bind the tear sufficiently. He had definitely been busy; and in light of his weaving, she admired his industrious nature. Delight studied him, tilting her head slightly.

"You are gifted," she whispered.

"Thank you, Lass. I wondered if ye intended to speak to me or possibly—"

"Douse you with the stew?" In truth the act had crossed her mind, teasing her hands until they tickled.

His blue eyes widened and he laughed, long and hearty. She liked this side of Henry, and he looked. . .well, rather pleasing. "You are blushing, Miss Delight. Me thinks ye had the thought rummaging about your head. I'm glad I spoke of it before I wore my meal."

Best you not know the truth for I'd be redder than the jacket of your uniform. She handed him the food.

"Thank ye, Lass. Sit down, please. Have you eaten?"

"Not yet."

"Would you care to join me?" Henry's tone indicated an earnest request, one that left her bewildered.

"I. . .I could fill a plate and sup with you." She wondered what the origin of her awkwardness might be. That strange sensation in the pit of her stomach assailed her again, as if she still traveled in the wagon and had hit a bump in the road.

"Splendid. I shall wait for ye and tidy up a bit around our spacious dining area."

Again that endearing smile. What had changed with him? She excused herself and returned a few moments later, but not without some jesting from her sisters about choosing to dine with Henry rather than her family.

"Never mind, daughters," Papa said. "She is conducting herself in a hospitable manner, and I find the trait commendable."

Delight relaxed in his defense of her. They had grown closer in the past few days, and she'd have been incredibly hurt if he'd allowed the teasing.

Once seated beneath the towering maple on a soft green blanket sprinkled with a few turning leaves of scarlet and gold, she noted the red color of Henry's hair blended with the early signs of autumn. She scurried through her mind for a topic of conversation. She didn't dare tell him about her and Papa's journey.

"Shall I give thanks?" Henry asked.

Delight bowed her head respectfully, eager to hear how a redcoat asked God's blessings.

"Heavenly Father, thank Ye for bringing my friends home safely. I have missed them."

Missed them? Delight's fingers trembled.

"Thank Ye for the continued healing of me leg and the craft Ye have given me to repay the Butlers for their kindness. Bless this food and the hands that have prepared it. In Jesus' precious and holy name, amen."

He prays just like the rest of us. How strange, and he didn't mention the war.

Henry picked up his pewter fork, soon to be melted down into musket balls. "I smell the changing season in the air, and from your house, apples and cinnamon."

"Mama does make delectable apple dishes. I was thinking about it myself—and all the preparations for the coming months." She nibbled at a piece of bread, conscious of his gaze upon her. Her stomach growled, and she fought the urge to devour the entire piece of bread, but those were inappropriate manners for a lady. "The nights are growing cooler," she added. "A welcome respite from the hot summer."

"I spent two winters in Canada, frightfully cold."

She nodded. "I suspect that must have been a hard life."

He glanced up from his food and caught her watching him. "All soldiers struggle with difficulties, Lass. The elements can be friend or foe."

She hastily looked away. This uneasiness between them must be attributed to only one thing. "Henry, we are not arguing."

He shrugged. "I gather it's because neither of us wishes to debate on our differences."

"I am too weary to contend about the war." Her admittance compounded the exhaustion pelting against her body.

"And I am too glad to see ye."

Her appetite immediately diminished. "Why did you say that?" She wanted to sound demanding, but instead she whispered the question.

He rubbed his chin with its weeks of growth. "I'm not certain, but it is the truth."

I cannot admit the same conclusion when I'm not convinced of my feelings. Oh, Henry, I would rather be quarreling.

They finished eating in silence while Delight tried to remember all those things she appreciated about the handsome James Daniels. That's where her musings should rest, not on a redcoat.

"Delight, I would like to discuss something with ye," Henry began. "While ye and your father were gone, I made a decision."

Her head spun, not knowing if she wanted to hear his findings. Perhaps knowledge of his subject matter would put her heart at ease.

From the house, Mercy and Hope raced toward them, waving and calling their names. "Papa is ready to play checkers with us and chess with Mr. Henry!"

ða

Henry waited patiently while Elijah pondered his next move. The master of the house had fallen under the luck of the Irish;

the patriot was three moves short of losing his king. They played by firelight, with the Butler family seated around and nary sputtering a word. Henry felt the family's championing Elijah in the silence wafting about the room.

On Elijah's right, the mistress held a tight smile. Her gaze wandered to the crackling fire, where she stared intently. No doubt her husband's role in the war kept her attention from the chessboard. She alone did not take the game seriously. On his left, Delight's sights fell on the sadly missing pieces of her father's side.

Be glad the fate of the colonies has not been decided in this game of wit.

His gaze could have feasted on her comely face forever, but he dared not relinquish his thoughts to his stirring emotions. First the family needed to learn of his discoveries, then he must make necessary plans. Only the advanced healing of his leg slowed him from making declarations this very night. Out of respect for Elijah and Delight's return home, he must refrain from drawing attention to himself. Although, if not for the precipitous arrival of Mercy and Hope, he would have told Delight of his prayerful conclusions earlier in the evening.

A smile lingered on his lips, not for the game but for the peace enveloping his soul. He loved this family with all of their quirks and pleasantries. Ah, Elijah truly led his household in a worthy manner, and the mistress held a silent strength. Noticeably, each young woman not only possessed worthy inner qualities but also outward beauty.

Delight had captured his heart and mind. She must have a sprinkling of Irish to love a good debate and fear not any game. Her oval face and flawless skin would hold any man's attention, and he dearly loved her spirit.

Charity, a vision of sweetness with not near the hasty tongue of Delight, held the qualities of a devoted wife and mother. Sometimes he wondered if deep inside the lass a resolute spirit grappled to surface. She always looked a bit pale, and Henry prayed God would keep her healthy.

Remember shared her faith in every word and act. Benevolent best described her nature. One day, she'd be a prize for the man who won her heart. Aye, he must have a servant's heart as well to do her proper.

Faith and Charity were both very much alike. They even resembled each other, more so than the other sisters with their freckled noses and sparkling smiles. Faith liked to cook, that one, and did a fine job.

Patience, the shy one. He had seen her slip away to put her thoughts into words. He viewed depth beneath those huge, brown eyes curtained in thick lashes like her mother and sisters. If he were not mistaken, quiet strength lived within her heart.

Mercy and Hope possessed the innocence that brought joy and laughter into each family member's life. They certainly had done so to Henry. When they lifted their angelic faces framed by a sea of lace in their mobcaps, he could refuse neither of them.

Again he stole another look at Delight. She must have sensed his scrutiny, for she met his quick look with a blush. If they were alone, he'd be hard pressed not to steal a kiss. Suppressing a chuckle, he could imagine her incensed reaction to such a bold act. When the time came to say good-bye, he would miss her sorely. How could a man lose his heart in so short a time? Even so, he'd found a higher purpose in the cause of freedom.

Finally Elijah moved his rook. "Henry, it is a powerful affliction to lose a game of chess in my own house, but I wouldn't want you to lessen your wit."

Henry chuckled. "Are ye sure ye want to move that piece, Sir?"

Elijah looked up, his gray eyes peering into his opponent's. "Is that a strategy? I'm thinking you are pushing me to make a different move."

"Aye, I am." *God is my witness; I have a weak spot for those destined to lose.*

"The rook stays."

The women were silent as they huddled around Elijah.

Henry moved his knight and took the rook. Elijah groaned, left with only a bishop and king. His next move put his king in check. "I believe I'm a beaten man," he said. "My king is doomed."

"Such a sad state of affairs, but I have always favored this game, and ye played well, my friend," Henry said.

Elijah clasped his hand on his shoulder. "You are a good man, Henry O'Neill, no matter what color uniform you wear. You took my king in a befitting game."

Elijah took a deep breath. Courage nearly escaped him. "You should have won. Americans fare better without the rule of royalty." He rose from his chair. "Good night, dear people. May you sleep well."

eight

For a long moment, Delight believed she had misunderstood Henry. Wonder at what had transpired in her absence danced across her mind. She glanced about the room. Papa's mouth stood agape. He, too, must be evaluating Henry's words. Illuminated hope from her father's prayers, of which she had only half attended, lifted her spirits.

"Henry, would you care to elaborate?" Papa asked hoarsely.

He turned and faced them all, lifting his chin with an air of pride. "Sir, I don't want to dampen your first night home with a matter about me self."

"Indeed, if I heard correctly, greater jubilation than our return has blessed this family."

Delight watched a myriad of emotions crease Henry's face. Even in the faint light, she could see his eyes mist. Was this what he wanted to tell her earlier? She braved forward, curiosity propelling her words. "I would like to hear what has transpired."

Only the sound of the clock ticking from the parlor graced her ears. Henry's gaze seemed to sweep from one person to the other, finally resting upon her.

"Perhaps Henry doesn't need such an audience," Papa said.

"I agree." Mama stood from her chair beside him. "Come along, girls. This has been an exhausting day, and I think it is time we join young Elijah in our own beds."

"I will accompany you," Papa offered. "In addition, my dear Elizabeth, you and I have a matter of our own to discuss."

"Aye," she said, her skirts bustling around the table. "I fear I may already know."

Poor Papa, but then again Mama might have steadied herself for the inevitable. Delight took her leave of the departing group in silence, certainly a trait uncommon to her. She smiled at each one, offering an embrace and words of love before they mounted the stairs. Not one teased or asked why she alone should be privy to Henry's words, although she hoped each thought her nursing position gave her the right to hear whatever tormented him.

Noting her clammy hands, she rubbed them on her apron and methodically placed the chess pieces back into an engraved wooden box.

"I was so distracted that I'm not sure how I defeated your father," Henry said softly.

She avoided his stare while a blundering loss for words added to her discomfort. Finally she spoke. "He rarely loses. You must be well versed in the game."

"Delight." His voice soft, laced with warmth and a spark of tenderness, sent chills to her toes.

Startled by the change he evoked in her, she lifted her gaze to meet his. Unable to speak, she listened to her heart pound furiously against her bosom.

"Could we converse outside? I know the evening's a bit cool, but if you don't mind—"

"The night is pleasant, but I shall take a shawl nevertheless."

Henry reached for his crutch just when she sought to hand it to him. Their fingers touched, and she hastily pulled back as though she had been burned. Perhaps she had.

They stepped into the chilly night air, and he closed the door. The creaking hinges and the singing insects sounded soothing in a strange way. Delight swallowed hard. *Help me, Lord, for I know not how to act or what to say.* The realization that Henry might no longer be her enemy both excited and alarmed her. The unknown, that is what she feared.

"A stroll would be pleasant," she said. Placing one foot in front of the other gave her something to do. Without movement, she would most assuredly dissolve into a pool of emotions she did not comprehend. Her anticipation closely resembled the cherished moments when her younger sisters accepted the Lord as their personal Savior, although nothing could compare to knowing a loved one embraced the Lord.

Bear joined them, loping along on the other side of Henry. She wished the dog had elected to separate them; at least she could have afforded herself some comfort with the animal between them.

"God has been speaking to me," Henry finally said. "I confess I may have made a tragic error."

"In what way?" If her heart beat any fiercer, it would surely burst.

"With the aspirations of this country, especially with the patriots' cause."

"Are you certain you want to be telling me rather than my father?"

"I believe he already has assessed my heart."

"Then, pray tell, what has God spoken to you?"

He clasped one hand behind his back and took a few more awkward steps before speaking. "Ye know my homeland in Ireland is poor. There is no hope for a man in me low estate to better himself or own land. Although me father has an honorable trade, he has never made enough to take care of all our needs. Always the taxes. Always the hard work."

Henry took a deep breath. "Here in America, I see a man's fondest dream of securing a bright future—hope of owning a prosperous business and feeling pride in his endeavors. I mistakenly believed the British had a right to make monetary demands—or any other mandate—on their colonies. But when I reflected upon me home, the poor drafted into the army, how one is born into a permanent station in life, I grew furious at the unfairness of it all. Here in America, I sense victory over oppression regardless of heritage."

Undoubtedly an answer to prayer, Delight silently acknowledged. She looked up at him and said, "Your words are true. Those are the things for which we strive."

"But I grew angry with me treacherous thoughts about Britain and wondered if me conclusions were simply unfaithful to the king. Indeed this poor man who hungered for liberty. . ." He paused. "Am I making sense, or am I rambling on?"

Still trembling, she admitted, "I understand you perfectly."

"The problem has been me friend Adam, who was killed just before I received my injury. I wanted the patriots to pay for his death, and I sincerely felt me sympathy for your cause meant he died in vain."

Delight sensed the grief he bore. It troubled her spirit, touching her heart as though God wanted her to feel Henry's intense pain. "I am so sorry. I've been guilty of thinking the British were all animals—hating them with no more provocation than seeing the uniform on their backs."

"And I've sinned with the same beliefs about patriots, but me mind has conformed to what I now believe is God's choice for me life."

She stopped in the middle of the road. "And how did this happen?"

"Sweet Remember acted as God's messenger, an angel in her own right." She heard the smile in his voice. "The first day I hobbled out to the maple tree, she asked if I wanted to read. She brought me a Bible and another curious book by the title of *Common Sense.*"

Delight giggled and covered her mouth. "Oh, my. How very much like me."

He joined in her laughter. "I thought she had brought me a novel, something in which to lose my worries. I began reading, and time slipped by. Everything I have ever secretly felt or desired was written within those pages, as though the diary of my longings had taken form."

"And did you struggle with what Mr. Paine recommended?" She considered how she would feel if a dear friend had fallen prey beside her and the enemies' beliefs suddenly become her own.

In the darkness, she saw him nod. "Aye, and I still do, but God, in His mercy, has shown me that liberty and freedom are due all men. I sorely miss Adam, but he is in a better place where freedom is not a question that bleeds a man's soul. No longer are ye rebels in my eyes, but patriots worthy of God's blessings."

Delight felt her eyes moisten and a single tear trickle down her cheek as her throat constricted with the overwhelming stirrings in her heart. "Papa and I have prayed for this, but I've not been a good example of our Lord. I gloried in your pain and hated you for what you represented."

"Neither have I pleased Him, urging ye to quarrel with me."

She hesitated. *Lord, I know not what Thee intends in Thy great plan.* "What shall we do now?"

"Friendship, perhaps?"

"I would like a good friend."

"This is splendid, and I hope our days of bickering are finished. I promise to do me utmost to prove it so." His words were punctuated with sincerity.

"And I as well, although I shall miss our debates." She laughed, and he joined her.

"I met a neighbor in your absence, Mistress Rutherford."

Delight could not think of one compliment regarding the woman. "She's. . .she is an unusual woman."

"She enjoyed my company until she discovered me reading Mr. Paine's book."

"What did she say?"

"Well, Lass, she was familiar with his writings and less than pleased with me."

Remembering Abby Rutherford's surly disposition, Delight imagined the woman's response. "Neither are we among her favorite people."

"I know with a certainty that if I ever desire a heated argument, I need only to knock on her door."

Again they shared a laugh, and it shattered the wall of past tensions between them. They walked farther, Henry limping along and Delight keeping pace beside him. Her thoughts raced with so many notions about this man. What would he do once his leg healed? And what of this new. . .friendship?

Logic gave her no peace. For once Henry's leg mended, he would be gone, but where?

≈

Although the night had a crisp edge to it, Henry felt uncomfortably warm. He wanted to tell Delight first of his revelation, but now that he had, he didn't know what to expect from her. An air of foolishness swept over him. This woman had no concept of her effect on him, and she might make light of it if she did suspect his growing feelings.

Friendship, he'd suggested. And she had agreed. Rather he continue voicing his plans for the future than speak too soon and face rejection.

"Once me leg heals completely, I will need a new uniform," he remarked.

The soft thud of his crutch against the road sounded as calming as the creak of a rocking chair against a wooden floor. "Blue is much more pleasing with your hair than red." She laughed, and her mirth eased his anxiety.

"My whole family, even my mother, has this color of hair! Dare you criticize it?" He couldn't hide the jesting in his voice.

"I shan't find fault in the substance, Henry. It is the unusual shade that I speak of." She brought her finger to her lip. "I believe Papa would gladly accept any color of hair, since he has nary a strand."

"Poor Elijah. I assumed living with eight women would cause any man to lose his hair."

She started to scold, but once again the two broke into laughter.

"I like the sound of your laugh," Henry said, "like the sound of a million fairies flutterin' about."

"You speak of fairies?"

"Little magical creatures from Ireland, Lass. Not real, of course, but I do know some who are not thoroughly versed in the Christian faith and believe folklore is true. They live and breathe leprechauns and such."

"Leprechauns?" She laughed again.

"Wee elves living in only me homeland, and if ye catch them, they will reveal hidden treasure." Whenever he spoke of Ireland, his brogue thickened.

"Do you miss home?"

"At times. I knew when I enlisted that I might never see me dear family again, but I'd love for them to see America."

"A pleasant thought. Perhaps someday they will."

"Perhaps they will. I would like to see the look on their faces at this wondrous land."

"Henry, are you sure about. . .changing sides?"

He heard the hesitation in her voice. "I would be a turncoat." He didn't feel remorseful; he merely stated a fact. "But rather a turncoat from the British than a man hindering the freedom of another."

"I am proud of you."

His heart seemed to swell. "Thank ye, Lass. God gives every man a call on his life; mine appears to be this one."

❧

The next two weeks found Henry growing stronger. Once a soldier stopped by to check on him, a friend who took the time to give him news about the war. He assured Henry that within weeks he would join up with the fighting again. Henry said nothing of his new allegiance; all would know the truth when his leg healed.

Every day he relied less on his crutch, until the morning arrived when at last he could cast it aside for a limp. Along with his healing came an enthusiasm for life—a vigor that gave him fresh hope for the days ahead. He abandoned his uniform for a tricorn hat, a white blouson shirt tied at the neck with leather pieces, brown breeches, and white woolen socks with his boots. Soon—much sooner than he desired— he must enlist in the Continental army. Not that he didn't want to fight for the cause; he simply loathed the thought of leaving Delight and her family.

He believed she didn't realize his true feelings, but her sisters whispered things that caused her to blush. Before he left their loving home, he must reveal his heart and take the chance of her rejection.

The people of Chesterfield learned of Henry's weaving and kept him constantly in their employ. He gave every bit of his earnings or barter to Elijah. After all, it was the least he could do.

The pattern of life became predictable. Predictable, that is, until Saturday, October 4, when a lone rider pulled a magnificent black stallion to a halt in front of the Butler home. Henry glanced up from his loom, taking in the noble stance of both horse and man.

"Good day, Sir," the stranger called.

Henry returned the greeting and rose to meet the man. Elijah was off delivering a barrel, and the women were alone. "Can I help ye?"

The man tied his reins around a hitching post and sauntered Henry's way. "I am James Daniels, looking for Elijah Butler. Is this his home?"

Henry extended his hand. "Aye, Sir, that it is. I'm Henry O'Neill. Elijah is due back shortly. He had goods to deliver."

The dark-haired man grinned broadly. "Mind if I sit and visit with you while I wait?"

Henry gestured for James to join him beneath the tree and offered a jug of water. He seemed a pleasant fellow.

"Did you receive an injury from the war?" James lifted the jug to his lips.

Henry touched his thigh. "Aye. Though it is nearly well."

"What battle?"

"Near Stillwater."

"Blasted redcoats. But we're turning them now. I hear tell there is a new battle brewing up along the Hudson now. We will whip them this time."

"The patriots need a victory to keep up their spirits."

James leaned closer and peered from side to side. "I hear Burgoyne has had his fill of deserters. He's offering ten and twelve dollars for the return of every missing soldier."

nine

Delight and Mama spent all morning behind Aunt Anne's house, melting down pewter and lead from dishes, kitchen utensils, and various other cups and candlesticks.

Aunt Anne, a quiet lady, small in stature, with flaxen-colored hair and sky blue eyes, was certainly not the picture of rebellion. She tossed a candlestick that once had belonged to a grandmother from Germany into the kettle. "I daresay my proper grandmother would have fainted dead away if she had seen me do this."

"Do you have any regrets?" Delight searched her aunt's placid face.

"Not at all. If I were forced to carry a torch from room to room, I'd still melt down my candlestick." Her words were spoken quietly but with the forcefulness of a lightning bolt.

"Here is my contribution." Mama's eight pewter goblets fell with a plop. "Mother gave me those as a wedding gift. Aye, she'd have disowned me, I fear." She stirred the contents with a heavy stick, then straightened her back. "I'd rather use them to supply a patriot's musket than to drink ale taxed by the British."

Delight laughed. Her mother had a way with words that she envied.

Aunt Anne poured another kettle of hot molten liquid into a musket ball mold, and while it cooled, Mama and Delight constructed cartridges from the ones made the day before. Delight much preferred making the cartridges. She could see a finished product, ready to transport to the Continental army.

"Daughter, are you lining these up like soldiers in battle?"

"Precisely. I want to see how many of our men we are aiding." She pulled her sewing scissors from her apron pocket and cut several sections of paper to extend beyond a six-inch metal tube. Once they exhausted the paper, they would use fabric. "Every one of these I cut makes me feel as if I've increased our chances to win the war. It makes me proud— but in a satisfied way." The feeling was different than that which she'd had while running messages in Boston, but the work was a worthwhile endeavor, nonetheless.

Delight rolled the tube one inch beyond the paper's edge, then dropped in a musket ball on the end where the paper overlapped and tied it tightly with twine. Holding the paper and tube securely, she poured in an explosive powder, pulled out the tube, and tied that end.

"I wonder what the British soldiers would do if they found us melting metal into musket balls and assembling cartridges?" Aunt Anne studied what they had completed.

Mama chuckled while tying the powder charge on a cartridge. "They'd take them all for themselves and probably order us to make more."

"I would rather be shot by my own handiwork," Aunt Anne replied. Hearing baby Elijah cry out in his sleep, she stepped over to the cradle once used by her children and nudged it into motion. "How soon must Elijah leave?"

Mama's mood instantly changed; her facial expressions revealed the weight of her concern. "One more week to get the butchering completed. I cannot convince him otherwise, and sometimes I am not certain I should."

"Matthew is talking the same." Aunt Anne glanced up. "Joining the others in the fighting means so much to him. Like you, Elizabeth, I understand his longing, but I am still afraid. If only we didn't have to worry about their safety."

"Henry is anxious for his leg to heal so he can enlist in the Continental forces." Delight instantly regretted her words. They were talking about husbands; she and Henry were friends.

"And how do you feel about his decision?" Aunt Anne rejoined them as little Elijah drifted back to sleep.

Delight hesitated and took a deep breath. "I am proud for him. He is a good man, and I'm sure he will fight bravely."

"Is that all?" A half smile tweaked at Aunt Anne's mouth.

Delight ignored the implication and tended to the task of cartridge making. "We have begun a comradeship, and naturally I'm concerned about his welfare."

"Is that all?" Mama repeated Aunt Anne's question. When Delight's gaze flew to her face, no measure of teasing greeted her.

"What. . .what do you mean?"

Mama opened the musket ball mold and studied the metal to see if it had cooled sufficiently. She closed it abruptly, an obvious indication the contents needed to set awhile longer. "I see the way Henry looks at you; and although you may not be fully aware of your own sentiments, I see a spark of something more than admiration in your face."

Papa said nearly the same thing.

"Mama, I have nursed the man back to health, and we've come to know each other very well."

"Precisely."

"Friendship doesn't indicate anything more significant," Delight pointed out.

"But it is a beginning. Need I remind you to whom he sought to reveal his decision to desert the British? While you were gone with Papa, he was like Bear without Mercy and Hope."

"I've noted the same behavior in the times I have visited," Aunt Anne added. "Matthew's remarked about you and Henry, too."

Warmth flew to Delight's face, and she shook her head. "You are sadly mistaken. Look at all the quarrels we've had—"

"Before he chose the side of the patriots," Mama said.

"In addition, I have my mind somewhat occupied with another."

Mama lifted a brow. "Daughter, it is not wrong to care for Henry."

But I don't know how I feel. If I did, this discussion would not be so difficult. She lowered her head and stuffed a musket ball into the paper form. "I understand." She paused, then added, "While with Papa, I did meet a pleasant man who said he planned to visit here soon."

Mama shrugged. "He captured your heart in one meeting?"

The conversation made her uncomfortable. "No, not at all. He's simply been in my thoughts."

"You are as stubborn as your father," Mama muttered. "Before we married, he told my sister his feelings for me were merely friendship and he could never imagine anything more. Three days later he spoke with my father about a possible marriage."

Aunt Anne laughed. "How well I remember. Although Matthew and I were young, we enjoyed the story."

But Henry and I are not you and Papa. We have said too many cruel things to each other to contemplate. . .consider. . . a mutual attraction.

But she'd seen the tenderness in Henry's eyes.

Mama hugged Delight's shoulders. "Forgive me for upsetting you. Affairs of the heart are never easy."

⋧

Henry conversed with James for almost an hour while they waited for Elijah. He continued to weave as they spoke about the war, the ongoing battle in Saratoga, the Continental Congress, and whatever other subjects the man fancied. James laughed easily—a good-natured lad in Henry's opinion. They commented about the pleasant weather and the fate of the troops in the winter months ahead.

"Under whom did you serve?" James finally asked.

A nearly ill sensation inched around Henry's stomach. "Me references are not of the utmost."

James peered at him in obvious question. "In what manner?"

Henry ceased working and eyed the man squarely. "I was a member of the British forces—a redcoat, a lobsterback—until recently."

Not a trace of emotion crept across James's face; neither did he utter a sound.

"The truth is, I got me self wounded at Stillwater, and soldiers brought me to the Butlers to mend. While here, I made some profound observations." He released a heavy sigh. "Me sympathies now belong to the American side. In short, I am a turncoat; and from what you said earlier, I have a price on me head."

James studied him for several long moments, as though searching for some mark of deceit—or so Henry surmised. "The British are combing the countryside, looking for their soldiers."

"I will be wary."

"May I ask what your plans might be once your leg is healed?" The words were simple, the implication deadly.

Henry stiffened. "Me allegiance is to the Continental army. I will join and fight alongside the likes of ye."

"The likes of me?" James's voice rose. He clenched his fists and stood from the hard ground.

I am no match for a well man. If he desires a fight, I shan't be in worse condition than the day I arrived here.

A slow smile spread over James's face, and he stuck out his hand to grasp Henry's. "I would be proud to stand against the British with you. You have courage, Henry. It takes a brave man to admit he's wrong and do something about it."

He laughed easily. "Then sit down, James. I am a bit uneasy with ye towering over me with your fists drawn."

James's laughter echoed around them, and once again he seated himself and talked on as before.

"Tell me, Henry, what do you know about Elijah's daughter? I met her two weeks ago and haven't been able to rid her face from my mind."

Not me Delight! Henry sought to resume his work, but his fingers refused to work together. *Could it be James and I are destined to be foes clamoring for Delight's affections instead of friends?* "The Butlers have seven daughters."

James shook his head. "I did not hear her name. She has light brown hair, large eyes—most likely brown, for it was dusk and some things I could not tell."

"Your description fits them all, and they are all quite comely."

From the two-story house came Mercy and Hope racing

toward them. "There are the two youngest now." Henry beckoned to the girls and a moment later introduced them to James. The girls curtsied and politely greeted the man.

"My sisters, Charity, Remember, Faith, and Patience, have prepared a noonday meal," Mercy said. "Would you care to join us?"

"Thank you, I will indeed," James responded. "I'd like to meet all of your family."

But not me Delight if I can help it.

Hope offered a grin, displaying two missing teeth. "Papa will be home later, and Mama and Delight are at Aunt Anne's." She nodded, punctuating her words. "The baby is with Mama."

Henry awkwardly pulled himself up from the loom, his leg stiff from sitting all morning. If he had any luck at all, Elijah would return shortly, and James would venture on his way before Mistress Butler and Delight found their way home. Even better, perhaps James would find himself enamored with one of the other young women of the Butler household.

The moment Henry and James entered the kitchen, Charity began to blush, and James could only stare at the young woman.

James leaned over to whisper, "You were right, uh, about their pleasing appearance." He removed his hat, and Patience invited him to sit at the table while Faith set an extra plate, Remember added a mug, and Charity sliced a generous hunk of fresh-baked bread. Viewing all that transpired, the guest wore a constant smile.

An inward chuckle threatened to surface in Henry. With a stroke of God's mercy, his Delight would not move James in the slightest.

Elijah arrived shortly after Henry pronounced grace and took over the duties of entertaining the guest. Between Elijah and James, Henry heard quite a bit of news about the successes at Saratoga.

"General Arnold did an outstanding job," James said. "But there is a riff there with General Gage. Undoubtedly, if

Arnold had received the reinforcements he needed, we would not have had to withdraw and instead would have given the British a good whipping."

"The battle is not over," Elijah reminded him, "and with a taste of victory, we will run those redcoats back across the Atlantic."

"A good many of them are homesick and disillusioned," Henry said. "The situation here is not what we expected."

James looked at him with an air of appreciation. "You, Henry, know better than most the morale of the troops."

"Many of us thought we'd get here and the rebellion would be put down in a few months. We also believed there were very few patriots, and the loyalists were eager to join our forces."

"I fear it will be a long while before America finds its freedom." Elijah set his mug on the table. "Fine meal, my daughters. The cottage cheese and bread were quite tasty."

"I agree," Henry said.

James echoed his praises, and once more Charity blushed scarlet.

"James, will you be staying with us this night?" Elijah asked.

"No, Sir. I need to ride on to Rutland before the afternoon is done."

"I would like for you to meet my wife. Are you of the mind to take a walk to my brother's home?"

Henry held his breath, wishing most intently that James would refuse Elijah's offer; albeit good manners prevailed and the guest agreed. "And your other daughter is there also? The young woman I met two weeks past?"

"Most assuredly." Elijah winked at Henry. "Would you care to join us, Henry?"

He knows precisely what is happening here. Elijah Butler enjoys the game of matchmaking—too much. I fear James and I will be a source of amusement for him.

"Indeed, Sir. This leg needs a bit of stretching out, and the walk will be refreshing."

ten

Delight counted the number of musket balls remaining and proceeded to cut fabric to form the cartridges. She had used all of their paper earlier and now resorted to the scraps before her. Holding up a strip of cloth, she turned to Aunt Anne. "I remember the dress you made from this."

Her aunt smiled and reached out to touch the pale green fabric. "The remnant still serves a good purpose, although I never fashioned it as a covering for a cartridge." She stared at the other pieces spread out on the ground. "Neither did I consider the cloth used for Matthew's shirts or my children's nightshirts."

Mama planted her hands upon her hips. "I daresay, we never thought we'd be melting down our pewter and iron for musket balls, either." She reached down to stroke baby Elijah's cheek with her finger. "But freedom requires a large toll."

Delight sensed her mother's sadness in Papa's approaching departure. For Mama, that knowledge must stand foremost in her thoughts. Delight wondered how she would feel if the man she loved intended to leave for war. Understanding Papa's not-so-distant journey to the Continental army saddened her enough.

The sound of men's voices alerted her. She quickly glanced at what they'd been doing and deemed it impossible to hide their workings.

It cannot be loyalists or British soldiers!

"I believe it's Elijah's voice I hear, but I cannot distinguish the other man." Mama released a ragged breath. Her face had turned a ghastly shade of white. "We should have devised a way to conceal what we have been doing."

Aunt Anne nodded, and she trembled. Delight's aunt seldom raised her voice or spoke openly in a crowd. Delight searched for something soothing to say, but with her ears strained to listen and a myriad of fears sweeping through her mind, she could only place an arm around Aunt Anne's thin shoulders. Suddenly Delight remembered the night she'd delivered information to Cavin Sullivan when the British soldiers pounded on the door of his tavern. She'd had nightmares for weeks following that frightful evening. Glancing about, she saw this fear now filled Mama and Aunt Anne.

"Elizabeth!" Papa called out.

Unaware of holding her breath, Delight let out a sigh of relief. *Thank Thee, merciful Father.*

"We are back here," Mama called.

Delight saw Papa move alongside the house with Henry behind him. He maneuvered fairly well without his crutch, his limp gradually becoming less profound. Then she saw him: James Daniels. Her knees grew weak, and she felt her face grow warm. The man indeed struck a fine pose.

"My dear Elizabeth." Papa waved at the fire heating the kettle full of metal and the other signs of what they were doing. "In the future, please use some discretion. We could have been the British." He shook his head, then offered her a light kiss to her cheek.

"The thought occurred to us too late," Mama replied. "Forgive me for alarming you."

Silent concern passed from Papa to Mama. He turned to greet Aunt Anne. "Good afternoon. You three have done well this day." He lifted Delight's chin and for a terrifying moment, she thought he might comment on her reddened face. "You above all should have used caution."

Why me? Sometimes Papa confused her.

"Elizabeth, I would like for you to meet a fine man here, James Daniels."

Mama curtsied and offered a welcome.

"Thank you, Ma'am. Your daughters prepared an admirable noonday meal, and I am beholden to their kindness."

Was it her imagination, or did he cast a sideways glance at her? If anyone could paint the portrait of the most handsome man in America, surely James would be the subject.

"I'll be certain to tell them so." Mama looked obviously pleased. Had she been smitten by James's charms as well?

"This is my sister-in-law, Anne Butler."

Aunt Anne appeared to be calmer than Mama, but shy nevertheless. She curtsied and offered a faint smile.

"And this little one is my son," Papa continued, "another Elijah."

James peered into the cradle at the sleeping baby. "A fine young man, Sir."

"And do you remember my daughter, Delight?" Papa grinned broadly, and again she felt her color mount.

"I remember the lovely woman I met two weeks ago, but I did not know her name. It is indeed a pleasure to see you again, Miss Butler."

She curtsied, feeling extremely awkward. "Thank you, Sir." Sensing someone staring at her, she stole a look at Henry. He did not look pleased. *We are simply friends. He should be happy for me.* But the voice in her heart revealed Henry's true feelings.

"James must be leaving soon, but I wanted him to meet you." Papa wrapped his arm around Mama's waist and laughed. "Thankfully, all of my daughters resemble their beautiful mother."

"Indeed they do," James said. "How fortunate for them."

Papa and James shared a hearty laugh, but Delight cringed and Henry gave a tight smile. She caught James's gaze, hoping she did not faint away with him before her.

"It has been an honor spending these hours with you and your family," James said, "but I must be getting along. I have a lengthy ride ahead of me and business to attend."

"Do come back," Mama invited.

"I shall, and I will look forward to visiting with all of you soon." He made pleasantries to Aunt Anne and then to Delight. "Seeing you again has been most delightful." He suddenly reddened, no doubt embarrassed at his choice of words, given her name.

She nodded and bid him good day.

"Are you ready, Henry?" Papa asked. "Can you manage another walk?"

"I believe I'll stay and help the ladies finish their work." Henry leaned against an oak tree. "I would like to see this completed and the evidence removed."

"Excellent idea."

Henry shook James's hand. "Thank you for the lively conversation. I look forward to many more."

Henry and James are friends?

James grasped his shoulder. "You are a fine fellow. I enjoyed your story, especially the ending. I'm glad you are on our side."

The guest walked away with Papa, then whirled around to Henry. "Do not forget what I warned you about; ten to twelve dollars is a great deal of money."

James is a pleasing man to look upon, but I don't know his nature. Could he possess Henry's wit and compassion? Delight wrestled with her thoughts. She had been drawn to James since their first meeting two weeks earlier, or was she drawn to his handsome appearance and the adventurous and dangerous life he led for the patriots? Surely all the women who were blessed by his presence felt the lure of his charm.

But what happens when the glow of adoration wears thin? She had no answers, for Henry held so many admirable traits that she found it difficult not to compare the two.

Delight wanted to understand what James had referred to in his closing words with Henry. Impatience wrapped its cloak around her while James and Papa slowly ambled toward the road. A leaf floating from the highest branches of a tree could not have moved more slowly. Finally they moved far enough away so that they could not overhear her question.

"What did James mean?" She picked up several pieces of fabric to show Henry how to form a cartridge. No point in exhibiting any more concern than she already felt.

Henry shrugged. "Nothing of importance."

She knew by the way he avoided her that a matter of great

importance plagued him. "Henry!"

"Delight," Mama scolded, "remember your manners."

"But he is concealing information from me." Irritation settled on her shoulders like a heavy yoke.

Mama cleared her throat. "In defense of him, I believe you are interfering with his private affairs."

Stunned, Delight could only stare at her mother. She had been disrespectful. Taking in a deep breath, she forced herself to face Henry. "I. . .apologize."

Instead of seeing condemnation in his blue eyes, she saw compassion and the clear distinction of something else. She shivered, captured by the tenderness in his gaze.

"I am not offended," he said. "I will tell ye what James referred to, and we can talk further about it on our walk home."

She nodded and blinked back an inkling of tears, of which she knew not the origin—nor was she certain she wanted to know.

"General Burgoyne is offering ten to twelve dollars for each British soldier brought in. Desertion has become a significant problem, and the general seeks to increase his troops."

Delight gasped, and her hand instinctively covered her mouth. "But they placed you here in Chesterfield until you healed."

Henry patted his leg. "This is healing much faster than I originally imagined. Very shortly, I will be able to do all the things I did before. The problem is. . ." His voice trailed off, and he picked up a few musket balls, toying with them as if they belonged to a child. "The issue at hand is the fact that I no longer feel any allegiance to General Burgoyne or to Britain."

He dropped one of the balls into the cloth form and picked up the gunpowder. "Of course ye already know my convictions on that matter. I need to enlist in the Continental army before the British lay claim to me."

"But—"

Henry raised his hand in protest. "We will continue this discussion later."

Mama and Aunt Anne laughed lightly, for it took a strong hand to silence Delight, and she knew it. At times she wondered if Henry could be more stubborn than she. And she truthfully didn't mind when he took the upper hand—not of late, in any event.

❧

Papa prepared to leave for the war on October 24, 1777, seven days after Burgoyne surrendered to Gates at Saratoga. Delight's father was determined to serve under the general who had forced the British to drop their arms. They heard the news from James Daniels, who happened to pass by Chesterfield late one evening.

His handsome face and proud carriage still took Delight's breath away. Sitting in front of the fireplace, he struck an overwhelming pose with the light from the rising flames framing his head. When she turned so he wouldn't see her face, she caught a glimpse of Charity, whose cheeks blushed brighter than a shiny apple. *My sister is taken with James, too?* She stole a glance at James. For a moment she thought he held Charity's gaze in his sights. *How dare you, Charity, turn this man's head when I had not decided whether to set my cap for him?* Frustrated, she attempted to listen to Papa's and James's conversation.

"I'd like to think we are going to end this war soon," James said. "The redcoats got a taste of real fighting in Saratoga and now know what it feels like to surrender."

Papa laughed heartily. "I might not get to fire Brown Bess before all of Britain leaves American soil."

I hope so, Papa, for then none of us would have cause to worry.

James left soon after Mama insisted he eat a heaping plate of ham and beans. As usual, he thanked Mama and Papa for their hospitality. He neither spoke to Delight nor looked her way, which angered her immensely. But did she see something pass between James and Charity?

❧

The day before Papa left for the war, he drew each family

member aside to tell of his love and to insure encouragement for the days ahead. His visiting took most of the day and into the evening.

After rocking little Elijah, he lifted his gaze to Delight. "We have not yet spoken. I'd like to take a walk." He settled the baby into Mama's arms and kissed the top of his forehead. Mama whisked away a tear, and Delight pretended she did not see.

Silently they moved into the evening and ambled toward the road winding from the town.

"Delight, I am leaving a tremendous responsibility for you as the oldest. You've always excelled in taking care of the younger ones and assisting your mother, but I am afraid this will be the hardest time of all."

"God will help me." *I will not cry; I'll be stalwart.*

"Allow Henry to share the burden while he is still here."

"Yes, Papa."

"He is a good man, Daughter."

"Yes, Papa." Hadn't they discussed Henry's merits enough?

"Delight, is your heart torn between Henry and James?"

"I haven't given the matter enough consideration to be able to answer your question."

"Let me suggest you speak with God about the matter. I have a preference for you, but I would rather you hear it from Him."

"I'll devote more time to prayer and reading the Scripture," she replied. "Perhaps it is neither man."

Papa chuckled, his voice musical with the sounds of the evening insects. "Whoever steals your heart must first give his own."

"Yes, Papa." She leaned her head on his shoulder, longing to listen to his words until the sun rose.

A few moments later, he cleared his throat and slowed his pace. "Another matter needs to be remedied."

Her pulse quickened. "And what is that?"

"I want you to promise that you will not endeavor upon anything foolish or dangerous during my absence."

Her heart pounded furiously. "What do you mean, Papa?"

He shook his head and released a deep sigh. "I know about your activities in Boston—the things you did for the patriots."

She felt her strength drain away. "How. . .how long were you privy?"

"Since the beginning."

She feared her weakened knees would force her to the ground. "Oh, Papa, I am so sorry, but I could not tell you about carrying the messages." The realization he knew about her activities all along both alarmed and relieved her. Shame for the deceit plagued at her heart.

"Daughter, I lived in fear of your being caught. What were you thinking the night you crept out to Cavin Sullivan's tavern?"

Speechless, Delight could only wring her hands.

"I nearly killed those soldiers when they pounded on Cavin's door in search of rum." His voice rose with each word. "My daughter at a tavern in the wee hours of the morning?" he muttered.

"You were there?" she said.

"Child, I followed you when I couldn't find the message myself!" Papa grabbed her shoulders and swung her around to face him. She gasped. His tone softened. "I admire and respect your courage, but you were taking too many chances."

But I did it for our country! She swallowed hard, remembering the times when she'd sensed someone stood in the shadows watching her as she skirted about Boston. "Why didn't you reveal your knowledge?"

"Because I was involved more deeply than you, and I saw that you could get past the British when the rest of us would have been detained." He broke into a sob. "I am a selfish man to allow my own flesh and blood to face insurmountable odds."

Her heart nearly melted in a pool of tears. "You are not selfish. You love your country and seek its freedom."

He wrapped his arm around her waist, and the two walked a bit farther. "I saw in you a sense of pride in your country, and I realized you would do whatever you could to aid the patriots. Unfortunately, my love of freedom blinded me to making sure you were free from danger. I should have forbidden you to continue your work. Will you forgive me?"

Her heart seemed to wrench from her chest. "Papa, there is nothing to forgive. If we did not come first in your prayers, you would not have volunteered to help."

He leaned his head upon the top of hers. "I had been involved with the Sons of Liberty since the very first. I've debated with Sam Adams, Hancock, and the others, helped unload those three ships loaded with tea in Boston Harbor, and smuggled muskets and supplies to our troops."

His confession brought a surge of deep pride to Delight, but then a thought needled at her, one she could not dispel. "Am I the reason we fled from Boston?"

Silence prevailed until Papa spoke. "Indeed you are. Your mother knew about me, but I did not tell her about your daring work until we moved to Chesterfield. I have continued my responsibilities here, but fortunately your work has been curtailed."

"I wish I could do more." Her regrets riddled through her body. "Making musket cartridges doesn't give me the satisfaction that running messages offered."

Papa laughed lightly. "It will have to do, because I want your word you will not venture into anything dangerous during my absence."

Given the opportunity, she would do anything for the cause, but Papa demanded an answer. "What do you mean by dangerous?"

He stopped in the road. "Any act that threatens your safety."

She groped for words.

"Delight."

"I promise to do my utmost not to involve myself in anything. . .dangerous."

eleven

At dawn, the family rose to properly send Papa off to war. Mama kissed him lightly and gave him a miniature of herself. He laced a piece of leather through the top and tied it around his neck. Charity packed his knapsack full of biscuits, hard cheese, and dried beef. A wooden canteen swung over his saddle.

"I am so lucky to have such a fine family to see me off. Many soldiers don't have a horse, either. God is blessing us indeed."

Remember gave him her Bible so Mama could keep the family Bible with all their family history. Patience slipped a piece of paper inside, most likely a poem or possibly a letter. Faith made certain he had a mug, a few cooking utensils, and a pewter plate—Mama had saved it from being melted into musket balls. Mercy and Hope stroked the horse, obviously unsure of what to do to keep their tears at bay.

"Here is a powder horn. It belonged to me friend who was killed. I'd like for ye to have it." Henry shook Papa's hand and they hugged.

Delight knew the two men had discussed matters long into the previous night. They'd become fast friends, and Henry wouldn't be with them much longer, either.

Delight had shined Papa's boots with her tears and polished his musket until it glistened. All the talk about liberty and separation from Britain seemed to lessen in meaning in the face of Papa's leaving. The British occupation in Boston, Henry's abrupt arrival, and even the making of musket balls and cartridges had kept the war on the surface of her heart, the part ravaged with anger. But this event tugged at her very being. This was Papa who rode off in defense of his country and his beliefs, Papa who might not survive the ordeal. Suddenly the war became more than a challenge. The mutual struggle had snatched her spirit and left her vulnerable and afraid.

Biting back a fresh sprinkling of tears, she forced a smile and handed Papa his musket. He kissed her forehead and met her smile with one of hope and a special look meant just for her.

He held Mama close while she silently wept against his chest. "Soon, it will all be over, my dear Elizabeth, and then I shall be home."

"God be with you." Mama touched his cheek as if memorizing every beloved portion of his face.

Delight repeated the blessing with her sisters, blinking back the stinging wetness blinding her vision. "Hurry home, Papa."

He swung up onto the saddle and nodded toward Henry. "I thank you for last night's conversation. We have a kindred spirit, and I am appreciative of your friendship."

"We have much to do once the war is won," Henry replied. "And I will be lookin' after things until it's time for me to go."

A feeling similar to the time when she was a child and fell out of a tree rose in Delight. The jolt had knocked the wind out of her, just as now she was left breathless at the realization of the sacrifice required to win this war. The battles would not be won by those carrying messages through enemy lines, melting pewter and iron into musket balls, or nursing British soldiers to health, but by the blood of those emptying themselves for America's right to liberty. Delight had mastered the simple maneuvers; Papa had volunteered his life.

Papa waved, and his horse trotted down the road. Oh, that he might never need to fire his musket, but Delight knew better. Oh, that he might not be cold, wet, and go without food and water, but Delight knew better. Oh, that he might never see his friends and fellow soldiers perish, but Delight knew better. *Father God, bring him back to us unharmed. I beg of Thee.*

Once he disappeared from view, she gathered up her skirts and hurried across the field behind their house. She had to flee the dismal scene of Mama and the girls weeping. Scurrying up a little hill, she swept down across a tiny, gurgling stream, up another grassy bank, and under a grove of elms, where she sank to the hard earth in a heap of liquid emotion. Mama had always said she and Papa shared liked temperaments. As a little girl, she had tagged along behind him wherever he went. This time she'd been forced to stay behind. . .and wait. . . and pray.

"Delight."

Unaware of another mortal nearby, she lifted her head from whence the sound came. Henry stood before her, his face filled with compassion.

"May I join ye, Lass?" he whispered.

Too spent to argue or agree, she said nothing. He eased down beside her, favoring his leg and allowing it to stretch out before him.

"You shouldn't have followed me," she said with a sniff. "Your leg is not mended enough."

"It grows stronger every day." He handed her a handkerchief. "I stopped for this."

"Thank you." *Soon you'll be gone as well.* The thought made her nearly as miserable, but she shoved away its confusion. "Why did you come?"

Henry picked up a golden leaf and appeared to study its veins. "Thought ye might need to talk."

She lifted her head and met his blue gaze. "I don't know what to say about anything."

" 'Tis nothing wrong about grieving your father's departure."

His words served to open the floodgates of her soul again. She attempted to swallow the tears, but her efforts failed.

Henry drew her into his arms and held her close against his chest. "Go ahead and cry. It will make ye feel better." His embrace comforted her while she soaked his shirt with her weeping. After several long minutes, she became aware of his chin resting atop her head and his hand stroking her back as if she were a small child. Humiliation overcame her at the thought of allowing Henry to witness her sorrow. She pulled back, not certain what to say, if anything at all.

"Forgive me," she said. "I do not like others to see me distraught."

"There is no reason for an apology. I am your friend, remember?"

His words coaxed a smile from her. "I rather others not see my weaknesses."

He nodded to punctuate his words. "The last thing ye are is weak, Lass. At the very least, you are the strongest woman I've ever seen—and the most stubborn."

Delight found another smile curving her lips. "Like my papa."

"Aye, I believe so." He leaned back against the elm and pulled her next to the hollow of his shoulder. *Do not be refusing me this wee bit of holding ye. It may be all I have to cherish in the days to come when I can't see your face or hear your sweet voice.*

Her back remained stiff, but she did not pull away.

"Tell me about Elijah. In your eyes, what best describes him?"

She entwined her fingers and pressed them beneath her chin as though she planned a lengthy prayer. "He is a proud man, my papa. Decidedly stubborn and determined all of us should have the best of things—not wealth, but love and a sense of purpose in our lives. He never complained of so many daughters and not having a son but always claimed God gave him the utmost of everything."

Henry chuckled. *Indeed He has.* "I hope to have many of his fine attributes someday."

"You have many now," she whispered. A moment later she rubbed her palms together vigorously, no doubt embarrassed of her assessment of him.

"What is your fondest memory of Elijah, the one standing foremost in your mind?"

Delight tilted her head. "Without a doubt, I remember the

occasion." She smiled faintly. "Albeit I'm a little reluctant to tell you the story."

He afforded himself a light pat of her shoulder. "Tell me, please. I promise ye will feel better."

She clasped her hands together as though ready to offer a prayer. "And you promise not to laugh?"

He heard the hint of a threat, but he had been the target of her temper before and had lived through it. "I'll do me utmost."

She settled back against him. *Aye, the touch of her is heaven.*

"What I best recall is a time before Mercy or Hope was born, so I must have been about five years old. Mama had asked me to feed our dog—Bear's mother—but I was afraid of her. The animal stood as tall as my head, and I thought she might devour me if I didn't give her enough food. I hadn't told Mama or Papa about my fears because I didn't want to disappoint them."

I can see ye then as ye are now, always wanting to take care of things yourself, just like ye nursed me to spare your mother during her confinement.

"I wanted to ask Charity to go with me, but the fear of her being eaten stopped my invitation. I knew if Charity were lost, Mama and Papa would be very angry." She glanced up at him. "Charity did perplex me so, crying whenever she couldn't have her own way, so the thought did enter my mind."

Considering the two girls were often at odds, Henry didn't doubt her statement in the least. A smile tugged at the corners of his mouth. "Did the dog have a name?"

She nodded. "Grace."

Henry couldn't stop the mirth rising within him. "Do go on, Lass. I'm not teasing you. It is the dog's name that amuses me."

She sighed and moistened her lips, those lips he longed to kiss. "Mama had the bowl filled with milk and dried bread, and I nearly sloshed it over while I carried it outside. I kept hoping the dog would be gone, and all I'd need to do was set the food down and hurry back inside to Mama, but that didn't occur.

When Grace spotted me, she came bounding over. She looked like a huge creature ready to consume me. I screamed and dropped the bowl. Grace kept running, but I stood frozen to the ground."

Henry envisioned the frightened little girl, convinced she would be the huge dog's dinner.

Delight sighed. "All of a sudden, I felt Papa's strong arms scoop me up into his. I clung to him sobbing and would not let go. Tenderly, he asked me why I feared Grace, and I told him."

"What did he say?"

"He told me I was more important to him than Grace, and if I wanted, he would get rid of the dog. Grace simply wanted to play. Of course, I didn't believe him. So while he held me with one hand, he petted Grace with the other. Finally I lifted my head from his shoulder and saw the dog licking his hand and wagging her tail. Papa coaxed me to pet her, too. Finally, with my hand overtop his, I stroked her head. Every day after that, Papa and I went outside to visit Grace. After a few weeks, I learned the dog was not going to eat me at all, and she really did want to play. The first few times she licked my face, I panicked, but Papa called her wet splashes against my skin kisses, and somehow I managed not to mind those, either." Delight looked up at Henry. "Sounds rather silly doesn't it?"

"Not at all."

"Grace and I became fast friends."

"I am not in the least surprised."

She glanced down into her lap. "I have a habit of fearing those things that mean no harm and ignoring real danger."

"I have never meant to harm you," he whispered. With more courage than he ever imagined, he lifted her chin with his finger. Surprise illuminated her gaze, but he refused to back down. Slowly he descended upon the softness of her mouth, drinking in a light kiss and praying she would not find him repugnant.

"Henry!"

twelve

Startled, Delight peered up into Charity's astonished face. "You should be ashamed." Her sister's tone was laced with indignation.

Delight stammered for words. Up until a few weeks ago, she had never had a problem speaking her mind clearly—and quickly—with words that cut deeper than a sharp hunting knife.

"Papa hasn't been gone two hours and already you are behaving indecently. You are a disgrace." Charity wagged a finger in front of Delight's face; judgment seeped from the pores of her skin. "You should have lingered for Mama. Abby Rutherford stopped by to tell her Papa was bound for eternal punishment for joining the patriots."

Shaking her head to dispel the accusations and the neighbor's judgmental words, Delight fought the urge to tell her sister to mind her own affairs.

"And I thought you felt something for James. Now I see you are fickle. . .or are you toying with both men's affections?" Charity lifted her chin. "We all are going to church to pray with Mama. Looks like you need to be on your face repenting for your sordid actions." She crossed her arms over her chest as if to punctuate her declaration.

"I have done nothing to dishonor God or shame my family. You, sweet sister, are the one who is viewing matters as evil when I am innocent."

Henry rose to his feet. He appeared impassive, as though the hostility between the two sisters was nothing more than an exchange of pleasantries over a cup of tea. "Charity." The low timbre of his voice issued confidence and control.

I don't need him to defend me, Delight thought. "Henry—"

His look stopped any further utterances. It reminded her of Papa when he expected her to cease everything immediately and do his bidding.

"Delight longed for a solitary place where she could grieve your father's departure and the impending danger of war. I sensed her sorrow and followed for the sole purpose of offering comfort, which is exactly what happened here."

"But. . .you exchanged a kiss!"

"Precisely so. I initiated it, taking advantage of her weakened state, an action for which I sincerely apologize."

"Henry," Delight interrupted, "you must not shelter all the blame." She stared into his eyes and saw the tenderness she'd seen previously. A fluttering sensation jolted across her stomach. "I did not attempt to stop you."

"Nonsense, Delight. I am sorry for me bold actions."

Do you regret the kiss?

"Please." Charity's eyes brimmed with tears. "I shouldn't have lashed out at you. Mistress Rutherford acted so cruelly and was so self-righteous. Then you two looked. . .I thought—"

Henry stepped forward and touched her arm. "Ye are hurting, too. 'Tis nothing wrong with feeling as ye do with your father leaving."

Charity nodded, unable to speak for the tears rolling over her cheeks. Compassion overtook Delight, and she gathered up her sister into her arms.

"Forgive me," Charity said between sobs.

"I am not offended. We all are suffering from the reality of Papa joining the war, but quarreling is not the answer, and I can be the worst offender in that regard. I believe we must show our love for him by extending it to each other. Imagine Mama's torment." Delight's gaze fell on Henry, who seemed to be studying her. A smile passed between them. This time she felt no fluttering in the pit of her stomach; instead a strange and lovely warmth filled her being. In one brief moment, all thoughts of James Daniels vanished in a light that could never measure up to Henry O'Neill. *I love him; I sincerely do.*

"Shall we join Mistress Butler and the others for prayer?" he asked softly.

Charity lifted her head from Delight's shoulder and took the handkerchief her sister offered.

"It is a little damp," Delight said. "Henry gave it to me earlier, and I soaked it thoroughly."

"I shall merely find a dry spot." Her sister attempted a trembling half smile. "I can always use my petticoat as we did when we were children."

"Excuse me, ladies. If ye are considering such actions, then I will go on ahead." Henry chuckled, breaking the tension in the air.

"Oh, no." Delight raised a brow. "We need an escort." In the midst of laughter, she realized her affections did include Charity, the sister who had always vexed her so. She brushed the curly wisps of damp hair away from Charity's face and kissed her forehead. Just as Papa always did.

❧

Henry spent the next few days with one eye on the road and one ear listening for British soldiers. If caught, he'd be forced back into the uniform of the enemy and be required to wield a bayonet in front of those he'd come to respect. He told himself on more than one occasion that he'd fall to his demise before raising a hand to stifle the patriot cause.

Soon James would arrive. Henry planned to ask him about enlisting in the Continental army as soon as possible. His leg needed only a few more days to heal properly. In the meantime, he would pass his time weaving for the people of Chesterfield and treasuring every moment spent with Delight.

Dare I reveal the depth of my feelings before I leave? He believed she felt the same; he'd seen it in her eyes. During those times when he sat weaving outside beneath the maple, he dreamed of living out his days in America with Delight beside him. *Oh, God, by all Ye deem holy, am I wrong to ask for this fair lass? I want to love her as Ye have instructed in*

Your own Word—as Christ cherishes the Church. Hear me cry, Holy God.

Henry prayed God did not regard his plea as selfish, although he knew desiring something for himself held all those qualities. He prayed for this wondrous land, destined to one day be the greatest in all the world. With the ideals of the brave patriots, America's destiny could be no less. Here, if God willing, he would live out his life and one day raise a fine family.

"Henry?"

He raised his sights, knowing the sound of Delight's voice. Her tone held a soft repose when she talked to him, just as he envisioned the sounds of the choirs of heaven echoed through the universe.

"Am I interrupting you?" she continued.

"Nay, Lass."

"You looked so faraway, as though you held private sanctuary with God, and I surely did not wish to interfere."

"Truthfully, my thoughts were on the things of God." He rested his hands on his knee. "But I am finished for now. What can I do for ye?"

She slipped down to the leaf-covered earth beside him. A brisk breeze obviously coaxed a gasp from her, for she massaged her arms lightly. "Winter is coming." She wrapped her woolen shawl tightly about her. "Henry, you need an outer garment."

He laughed. "My coat is the British uniform. I believe I would rather be cold."

She glanced away, and he saw the visible traces of sadness etching her face. "I believe Uncle Matthew has an extra outer garment. I will fetch it today for you."

"How generous of you. But I don't have money to pay."

"He offered when you wove aprons for Aunt Anne."

He hesitated. "It is time I enlisted."

"I know," she whispered.

Is now the time to speak to her, Lord?

Not yet, My son. Wait for Me.

The clear direction caused him to bridle his tongue.

"See, you are chilled," Delight said. "I will get a blanket from inside to wrap about your shoulders until I return with a coat." When he protested, she raised her chin. "You can't do the patriots a bit of good if you are ill. I nursed you once, and I daresay you remember how difficult I can be."

"Nay, I remember an angel's touch." He could not stop a teasing grin. "One with eyes of fire."

She instantly sobered. "I am sorry for the way I treated you."

"Are ye now?" He forced a jovial disposition, sensing her melancholia.

"Yes, and do not make light of me. I will sorely miss you, Henry O'Neill." She anchored her hands onto her hips.

He wanted to pull her close to him and kiss her soundly; but he restrained his emotions, wondering if another impetuous act might displease God or anger her. "I will miss ye, too—everything about ye."

Silence invaded their small place. In the distance a dog barked, and birds sang above them as though everything about the world rested secure. Reality spoke otherwise. *Thank Thee, Lord, for moments of reprieve when the rest of the world moans and shudders.*

"Promise me you won't get hurt." She lifted her hands from her hips and let them dangle at her side.

Heaviness settled upon his shoulders. "That is impossible, Lass. Only the heavenly Father knows the future."

She drew in a breath and blinked hastily.

"But I will promise to heed caution and to serve the Continental army to me utmost."

"I expect you to exceed even those expectations."

"I am only a man guided by God."

"Then I pray He keeps you in the shelter of His wings."

Will ye prayers always include me? Dare I hope so? Henry swallowed the endearing words he yearned to speak. Silently he proclaimed his devotion until God willed him to make his declaration of love. He recalled the late-night conversation he'd shared with Elijah before his friend's departure.

"You have my permission to wed Delight," Elijah had said. "I can't think of a finer husband for my daughter or son-in-law for Elizabeth and me. My blessings, Henry. Aye, she can be a handful, but you will never find greater devotion."

"Thank ye, Elijah. I admit I don't know how she feels, but I know my heart."

Elijah laughed heartily. "Delight may not understand her own sentiments, but I do see your favor in her eyes."

Since then, Henry had looked intently into his beloved's eyes at every opportunity, hoping for a glimpse of love. At times he felt certain; other times he doubted she felt anything at all. Perhaps he merely read words into her silent messages or the tone of her voice.

"I did come to tell you something." Delight's voice broke into his ponderings. "Mama said James will be arriving by nightfall tomorrow."

⁊⁊

Delight left Henry in the cold air and walked back into the house to tell Mama about hurrying to Aunt Anne's for the promised coat. Taking a deep breath, she wished she could muster the courage to tell Henry that James meant nothing to her. But if she made the claim, then he would surely see her growing feelings for him. The idea of Henry not sharing the same affections sounded more devastating than not knowing his feelings at all.

Charity had admitted her fondness for James, and Delight had wished her God's blessing. How odd and yet wonderful that it took a misunderstanding to bring the two sisters closer together. All these years they had quarreled with and avoided each other, and now they were inseparable. Indeed they giggled and talked late into the night like dear companions.

"Henry does care for you," Charity had whispered just last evening while the rest of the house slept.

"Are you certain?" Delight's pulse quickened at the thought.

"Absolutely, without a doubt. He has eyes only for you, as though you hung the stars in the sky."

"Is that blasphemy?"

Charity sighed. "I pray not, for he is a godly man, and I sense his great love."

"Oh, Charity, if only he would speak to me about his feelings. I ache to hear any words of endearment." She shivered with the truth echoing through her. "Yet I am fearful if something should happen to him."

"What if he should leave without telling you?"

Delight felt her spirits sink. "Pray he speaks his mind before he departs."

"I will, Sister. I will with all the fervency in my very being. He would not have kissed you if he did not care."

"Thank you." Delight felt her eyes moisten. "I wish we could have become close long before this very moment."

"Aye, we've missed so very much. I always loved you, but our closeness now is beyond my deepest dream."

Delight felt deeply moved with the confession. "And I love you, Charity. Just like your name, you give in abundance. I will pray James sees your goodness."

Delight smiled at the remembrance of the sweet times lately with all of her sisters. Adversity had a way of ushering in God's grace.

Glancing at the huge piles of wood Henry had chopped in preparation for winter gave Delight a sense of relief. Her family would not go hungry; neither would they freeze in the cold. They'd have the company of each other to sustain them through the hard times until Papa—and Henry—returned. If only she had some type of assurance that Papa and Henry might fare as easily. She wanted to do something to help, but what? Helplessness wove its web of inadequacy, leaving her heavyhearted and frustrated.

She could not carry a musket, although she had heard stories of wives who followed the troops to cook and tend to the soldiers. Some, when they saw their husbands fall in battle, picked up their weapons and continued the fight.

She'd promised Papa not to indulge in dangerous activities, which meant in her estimation that she could do little of any value for the cause.

Where is your faith?

The whispers from a place neither her heart nor her mind could claim spoke with a truth she could not deny.

You believe in Me for eternity; why can't you trust Me with the present?

thirteen

The next evening, Henry waited with tumultuous feelings for James's arrival. The man had become a good, respected friend, and he valued their relationship. But what of the man's interest in Delight?

Loving her meant Henry desired the utmost for her, God's richest blessings. *I need to fade into the background and allow them to grow closer. I give her to Thee, Lord. My wish for her happiness exceeds my selfish ambitions.*

The afternoon came and went. Henry delivered woven goods to three families and took an order for one more. All the while he harbored mixed emotions about James's tardiness. Mistress Butler waited the evening meal in anticipation of their guest joining them, but at last they partook of the food. James was a man of his word. He lived a daring life; he would walk through Satan's fire if it furthered the cause of the patriots. His delay sent an uncomfortable sensation up Henry's spine. Surely the British soldiers and loyalists sought to end his life—a possibility Henry tried without success to push from his thoughts.

"James must have been detained," Mistress Butler said during the meal. A silence had befallen them. Even Mercy and Hope were unusually quiet. In their young minds, a word from their guest might be a word from Papa. "Shall we pray for him? Perhaps Henry would do us the honor."

What a blessing for me to lead this family in prayer, Henry thought as he bowed his head. *Thank Ye, Lord.* "Heavenly Father, we welcome Your presence into our lives, and bless Your name for these bounteous gifts. We humbly ask Ye keep careful watch on our dear friend, James. Protect him from harm's way and sustain him in the shadow of Your blessings.

Lord, also remember Elijah. Bring him through this war without injury and back to all of us who care for him. In Jesus' name, amen."

Once the firelight cast its shadows, the sisters closed the shutters and latched them. Mistress Butler fed the baby and rocked him to sleep, nearly drifting off herself before gathering up a basket of mending. An hour later after reading the Scripture aloud and practicing their writing, Mercy and Hope made the trek upstairs to bed. Some of the young women busied themselves with knitting or their samplers, while Patience wrote a letter to her father, and Charity kept one eye on the door. Delight said little, no doubt fretting with Charity over James's absence. She held a book in her hand, but not once did he see her glance at a page. Henry listened for every sound, anxious to hear Bear's bark, announcing a caller.

"I am certain James will be here soon," Henry said, long after the hour grew late. "Only his loyalty to the cause would hinder his presence."

"I agree." Mama put aside her mending. "I believe we should not tarry in obtaining our rest. If he arrives, we shall hear him."

Henry knew he wouldn't be able to sleep. The gnawing in his spirit had lingered after his prayer. "I believe I will resume the watch a wee bit longer."

"I should like to keep you company." Charity spoke from a corner chair where she had long since set her basket of yarn at her feet. "Delight, I would appreciate your presence."

"Of course. We can talk or read."

"Do not stay up too late, girls," Mama said. "Tomorrow is another day."

Henry noted the gentle smiles and compassion exchanged between Delight and Charity. His beloved had told him of their renewed dedication to each other, and he'd seen the change since the day of Elijah's departure. He wondered about their common attraction to James and how they could ignore their emotions. Rather than deliberate the matter, he quickly discarded it. After giving the worrisome problem to God, he shouldn't keep calling it to mind. Tonight his concerns belonged to James.

His friend had mentioned running provisions and ammunition under the guise of shelled corn in barrels that Elijah had constructed. If the British searched the contents of James's wagon, they would find more than corn to grind into flour and certainly end his friend's quest for liberty—and his life. None of those possibilities needed to be communicated to the fair women of the Butler household. He believed they should be sheltered from whatever unpleasantness possible, with the exception of Delight. Henry had a feeling she could see her way through just about anything.

Another reason why he loved her.

"What do you suppose has detained him?" Charity asked. In the next breath, she stood and paced in front of the fireplace.

"A number of things could delay him." Henry purposely kept his voice calm and quiet. "With his activity among the Continental forces, he is probably on a special mission." His answer held more truth than he cared to admit.

Charity nodded and forced a grim smile. "Of course. Tomorrow we shall be exhausted because we tarried into such a late hour."

She obviously cares for James. He glanced at Delight. Worry lines creased her forehead. How he longed to comfort the burden resting on her mind.

"James is self-sufficient. It is wrong for us to agonize over his absence. He would not want any of us to fret over this." Delight stood and placed a hand on Charity's arm. "Let's go on to bed. Bear will alert us."

Charity's shoulders rose and fell as if a heavy sigh had drawn her strength. "Aye, you are correct in your assessment." Her gaze lifted to her sister's face. "Come along then."

The two bid Henry good night and encouraged him to seek his rest.

"I shall, Lasses." He avoided Delight's face, knowing her

heart was with another. "Sleep well."

After the women ascended the stairs, Henry allowed his own thoughts to wander. James was not blind to the uncertainties of his position. He had a clever side to him that had kept him a step ahead of the enemy. Still, danger loomed in these perilous times, and Henry could not help but think of Adam and his other compatriots who had perished in the fighting. Henry wasn't ready to lose another friend, albeit he realized many fine men on both sides held death as their destiny before the war ended. He could be one of those, too.

Henry had given himself four more days before enlisting. In truth, he and James planned to travel together to the nearest camp, where his friend assured him of a proper introduction to General Gates. Regardless of where James might be at the end of the allotted time, Henry planned to venture on himself. They had spoken about a great number of things from their boyhood days to their understanding of God's salvation to war stories, but nothing about Delight. He assumed she was a subject neither of them wanted to broach.

Repeatedly Henry told himself God had a special woman intended for his life, and if not Delight then surely someone better. But he could think of no one finer than the woman who had stolen his heart.

"Henry?" the one holding his thoughts whispered behind him. "Do you mind if I keep you company?"

Warmth flowed through him. "Of course not. Ye cannot sleep?"

She shook her head. "Charity is resting, though, and for that I am grateful."

Poor Delight. I know the pain of a heart wounded by love.

With the flames licking at the log he had just added, she eased down to share his bench. "I thought we might talk since. . ."

He quickly captured her gaze and held it for as long as she permitted. "Since we are waiting for James," he said, finishing her sentence.

Silence permeated the air, and she stared into the fire. "Yes, that, too; but I meant we could converse since you planned to enlist soon."

How sweet to concern herself with me in light of her feelings toward James, he thought. "In less than a week, I will be serving under General Gates."

"Perhaps you shall see Papa."

"I'd like nothing better than to fight with him."

She toyed with the cuff of her frock. "I would be most grateful if you'd tell him of our love and prayers."

"Aye, Lass, I will. There's no need to ask."

"What do you intend to do after the war?" She peered into his face, her large eyes innocent and. . .did he see fear? "I assume you will want to continue your weaving."

"My loom is me livelihood, but I have a desire to live among the dear people of Chesterfield. Your father asked me to come back here."

She smiled. "We would all like for you to make your home near us."

He chuckled. "Delight, I remember when ye detested the sight of me, and now ye want me near your family?"

In the firelight, she blushed. "I remember, too. I am so glad those days are gone."

He memorized every inch of her lovely features. "Are there things you wish for me to do before I leave?"

"I think not. We are ready for winter, thanks to your and Papa's provision."

A strange, yet comforting silence fell upon them. He relished in it, promising himself these memories would warm the bitter winter days and nights ahead.

"I'd like to ask you something, Henry."

He raised a brow. "By all means."

Her gaze darted about, and she appeared to have difficulty forming her words.

&a

Why did I initiate this conversation? Delight cringed with what she so desperately wanted to ask, troubled over what Henry might reply. She had contemplated this for too long. The thought plagued her worse than enduring baby Elijah's cries when Mama forbid anyone to pick him up. She could not go on another day without knowing. Henry had acted so indifferently since the day Papa left. His impassiveness led her to believe he regretted his kiss. The notion of their brief embrace meaning little should have angered her, but instead the thought filled her with sadness.

"Delight?"

Oh, how I wish I had not pursued this matter. My mind should be on James and prayers for his safety, not myself.

"What is tormenting ye? I can see the anguish in your face."

The fire crackled, sounding like musket fire, and it caused her to gasp.

"Lass, it is only the fire."

"I know, Henry." She rubbed her clammy palms together. "Remember the day Papa left, when you followed me to the far field?"

He nodded.

"And Charity came looking for us?"

"I clearly recall every moment."

With a deep breath, she spoke the penetrating question. "Did you have any affections in your kiss?"

Henry leaned forward, his words spoken in a whisper. "Did ye?"

How can I answer without looking foolish? Dear Lord, this is difficult beyond measure.

Bear rose on his haunches and stared at the door. A growl rumbled in his throat.

"Easy." He stroked the dog's back. When the animal moved forward, Henry reached for the musket hanging above the fireplace.

Bear knows James; he'd never growl at him. The dog barked, and Delight jumped.

"Delight, go upstairs with your family," Henry ordered.

"Do not come down until I tell ye everything is safe."

She started to object, but the commanding tone in his voice stopped her from protesting. Still she did not move.

"Now! This is not a time to argue."

"You might need assistance."

Henry raised an angry brow, and she hurried up the stairs. Someone other than James approached the house.

Henry heard Delight's light footsteps up the stairs, but his sights remained on the door. The feel of the weapon in his hands gave him little reassurance. Those who roamed the night in search of mischief rarely came unarmed.

With one hand on Bear in hopes of keeping the dog quiet, Henry stepped to the window and slipped his fingers between the shutters, easing one side open to see outside. The culprit might simply be another animal roaming beyond the door, but Henry had a feeling this was not the case.

In the faint light of a half moon, he saw the outline of a wagon. The driver, wearing neither the uniform of a British soldier nor the varied garments of a patriot, leaned precariously to the side, as if inebriated or injured. Rather than open the door and possibly face trouble, Henry left Bear inside to protect the women. Releasing a heavy sigh, he stole out the back of the house.

Moving slowly around the rear to the corner, he considered how darkness often masked the sounds of night. The noises seemed to come from the distance—the singing insects, a bawling cow, and an owl's call. While he crept toward the front of the house, he strained to hear something revealing the wagon driver's identity. Nothing met his painstaking gaze. When he reached the front, he studied the wagon's outline. Not a soul loomed nearby, save the man, who looked ready to tumble to the ground.

Henry scrutinized the wagon bed and focused on the peculiar shapes filling the entire area. Barrels. The driver must be James, and indeed he must have been badly injured not to cry out. Bear must have sensed the calamity.

He moved to the wagon and worked his way around to the seat. Caution preceded his every breath for he knew not what might await him. "James?" A groan met his ears. The chap needed care, no matter who he was. Henry attempted to lift him in his arms while leaning against the wagon on his good leg. He feared dropping him; and with the man uttering nothing more than a whimper, the fall might kill him.

Help me, Lord. I need to get him inside.

Henry reached beneath the limp man and pulled him against his chest. He took a staggering step, determined to place one foot in front of the other until he could lay the man down within the house.

The door opened and captured his attention. Delight, carrying a lantern, rushed out with Charity. Instantly the two young women were at his side. Delight assisted with the man's legs and Charity held his shoulders and head.

"You are an answer to prayer," Henry said, "although I distinctly remember asking ye to stay inside."

"I watched from the window and assumed all was safe," Delight replied. "And I saw you needed help."

"Is it James?" Charity whispered.

"I do not know, Lass, but it most likely is. He's injured, but I don't know where."

"He looks like James." She caught her breath, no doubt halting her tears. "Delight, please shine the lantern."

Charity gasped at the sight of their friend, his face smeared with dirt and blood. A gash from his head oozed fresh blood.

"We'll tend to him and offer prayers." Delight's compassion sounded tender against the stifled sobs of her sister. "Don't worry, Charity. If he made the journey here, then he is strong."

Once inside, they carried him into the hall and placed him on Henry's mattress.

"Stay here with James," Delight said to her sister. "I will get a basin of water and see to bandages and herbs."

"Should we wake your mother?" Henry eased James's arm

from his waistcoat to make certain there were no other injuries. Charity knelt at his side and helped pull the coat under him while Henry lifted.

"Let's see the extent of his wounds first," Charity replied. She first saw the profuse bleeding from James's side when she pulled his arm from the other sleeve. "Oh, dear Lord, please spare him." She peered into Henry's face. "Mama will know what to do." Rising to her feet, she disappeared up the stairs, the wisp of her skirts reminding him of a humming-bird's wings.

While Henry sought to make James comfortable, Delight returned with water and a cloth. She knelt in the same spot where she had once dressed Henry's wounds. "How serious is he?"

Henry hadn't had ample time to assess his friend's condition, but he did know the bleeding from his side needed to stop. "I have to find the source of this blood—either a knife or musket ball."

Delight held the lantern, neither flinching nor commenting about the open flesh.

"A knife, Lass. His head, too. These need to be sewn or the wounds will not heal properly."

"Either Mama or I can do it," she said. "Blood usually makes Charity ill, but she may amaze us." Delight pressed the cloth to James's side to halt the profuse bleeding. Even so, red soon tinged her fingers.

Father, he is far worse than I imagined. "How could Charity's reaction vary from her disposition?"

Delight smiled sadly. "She loves James, and I'm sure she would do anything to help him."

Henry tore the remains of his friend's shirt away from the wound. *How can both of these women love the same man without quarreling? I don't understand their behavior, no, not at all.* It occurred to him that he and James probably cared for Delight. He thought of James as a brother. Perhaps there rested the similarities.

"Would you hold this for me, please?" Delight whispered.

He held the cloth against the open flesh while she gingerly washed the area around it. Tiny lines etched around her eyes while she concentrated on cleaning a small portion of the surrounding area.

"Thank you. I am afraid this isn't as simple as when you were injured."

"Aye, but I had a fine nurse." He refused to dwell on James's serious condition. As a soldier, he had learned the value of a clear mind.

"A surly one." She smiled faintly.

"She had a disagreeable patient."

Delight glanced behind them at the creaking stairs announcing Mama's and Charity's descent. The hum of their anxious voices intensified the critical situation.

"Mama, I have water and bandages along with yarrow, but one of us will need to sew his wounds," Delight said.

At the sight of the seared flesh illuminated by the lantern light, Charity covered her mouth. In the next breath, she righted herself and offered to retrieve Mama's sewing basket.

"Aye, I will need it," Mama replied. Henry helped her kneel at James's side.

Charity swallowed hard while tears rolled unchecked down her cheeks. With a quick breath, she whirled around to fetch the basket.

"We must make haste," Mama said. "Is he conscious?"

"I think he's drifting in and out, " Henry replied. "Only moans, and scant few of them."

"That is a blessing for now." Mistress Butler brushed her long, gray mottled hair back behind her ears. Normally, she wore it in a bun at her nape. "From the looks of James, he must have rolled in the dirt during some scuffle."

Mixed with blood, the debris caused the open flesh to appear even more gruesome. Mama took nearly an hour to stitch up James's head and left side. Her stitches were neat, whereas Delight knew hers would have been jagged and uneven. More than once, Delight stole a glimpse at Charity's face, but her sister did remarkably well. She held James's hand as if the man were conscious of her touch. Thankfully his state masked the painful sensations certainly raging through his body.

" 'Tis all I can do." Mama wiped her brow with the back of her hand upon completion of the task. "James's wounds will close and heal properly as long as fever and corruption don't claim him."

Charity stroked his forehead. Even in the dim light, he looked fearfully white. "We must pray."

"I will," Henry said. "Lord, we are all concerned about Your child here. He's hurt bad and needs Your help. Guide us in how we can help him. And Father, we pray no corruption shall plague James's body, but that Your power will touch him with divine healing."

He wondered what ill fate had befallen their friend. A thought occurred to him, and he mulled it over in his mind. What if James had been followed? Loyalists and redcoats alike did unspeakable things to patriots, especially those apprehended with messages and supplies. No one dare find any trace of James at the Butler home.

fourteen

"I will take care of the horses and wagon." Henry rose stiffly to his feet.

"I'll help," Delight offered, "as long as Charity will sit with James so Mama can rest." She needed fresh air and time to ponder James's ill fate.

"Of course." Charity reached to take Mama's hand. "Go on back to bed, Mama. Morning will come soon enough, and little Elijah will be demanding his breakfast."

Their mother studied James a bit longer. "Do you promise to waken me if he grows worse?"

"I give you my solemn word," Charity replied.

Henry assisted Mama to her feet and did the same for Delight.

"Would you like a cup of chamomile tea before retiring?" Delight asked.

Mama smiled wearily. "I think not. Once you and Henry are finished outside, perhaps you three would sleep intermittently in your vigil. Who knows what tomorrow will bring?"

"I'll see to it, Mistress Butler," Henry said. "Do not concern yourself with their welfare. I will make sure they rest."

And who will urge you to do the same? Delight wondered as she grabbed her shawl and wrapped it around her shoulders before grasping the lantern.

Once outside, Henry drove the wagon to the back of the house, where he could hide both it and the horses inside the barn. He pulled the barn door shut, and with Delight's aid, he fed and groomed the horses.

Delight leaned against the side of a stall. "Henry, you never answered my question earlier."

"I believe I posed the same to ye."

Her thin shoulders rose and fell. "Must you torment me so?"

Me dear Delight. It is I who is tormented. Henry looked at her steadily. "That is not my intent."

"Then were you trifling with me the day Papa went off to the army?"

Henry knew he must respond, and he dared not lie. "I am leaving shortly, Delight. I don't know when I shall return, but I assure you my kiss was with the utmost of affections."

Delight realized her desire for Henry's reply was selfish in light of James's grave wound, but nevertheless she warmed with the sweet words. "Thank you, Henry. No one has ever given me such a lavish compliment."

"After tonight, perhaps we might talk?" His tone sounded wistful. "I mean once we are certain James is on the mend. I'm ashamed of myself for concentrating on my sentiments instead of placing my heart and mind into our friend's care."

She glanced up and nodded. "I understand how you feel, but God does not expect us to grieve continuously."

A brief silence followed when she could think of nothing to say.

"I want to see what's in the barrels," Henry said. "I know James has been smuggling supplies and provisions to the troops for some time. My guess is someone wanted what he carried."

He climbed onto the wagon and pried open one of the barrels with a crowbar. Delight held the lantern high, anxious to see the contents.

"Corn," she whispered as Henry allowed the kernels to flow between his fingers. The sight somewhat disappointed her.

"Quite possibly there is something else in the bottom." Henry dug his hand deeper, nearly to his elbow. "Ah, Lass. We may have a treasure here. Do you mind fetching me a bucket?"

Once the desired item was obtained, she climbed onto the wagon bed beside him. Quickly he scooped the corn until his knuckles rapped onto a hard surface with a dull thud.

"What do you think it is?" she whispered, as though they were being spied upon.

"I think I know what we have here." He pulled a wooden insert from the barrel. "Hold back the lantern, Delight. It's gunpowder."

She stepped away from the wagon and drew in a deep breath. So this was why James had been attacked. "Henry, this needs to be delivered somewhere."

"Indeed, but until James regains consciousness, we can only speculate where. I searched him but found nothing. Didn't really expect to. James is too sly to carry vital information on his person."

Delight well understood that precaution, which was one of the reasons she had assisted the patriots. Papa said James could read an item once and memorize it, definitely an asset to their cause. "I would gladly drive this wagon to its destination."

Henry replaced the wooden insert and picked up the bucket of corn. "I thought Elijah made you promise you wouldn't involve yourself in any dangerous activities."

Irritation piqued her, although truth be told, she had momentarily forgotten her promise. "How did you know about that?"

He poured the corn back into the barrel before replying. "He sensed you might have a difficult time keeping your word."

"I believe he would make an exception in this case."

"I think not." Henry replaced the barrel's lid and climbed down from the wagon. "If he had not felt concern for you, then he might not have alerted me to your promise."

She tapped her foot against the hard ground. "How else will it be transported?"

"I believe I'm quite capable."

"But your leg?"

He moved closer to her and took the lantern. "Is the question my leg or my loyalties?"

Stunned, Delight wrapped her arms about her. "I don't

doubt your commitment to the patriots, but I had not considered you—"

"Risking my life for the American cause?"

The conversation vexed her, forcing her to consider things she hadn't mulled in her mind before. "Forgive me, Henry, but this is all new to me. First you tell me what Papa made me promise, then you announce your willingness to continue James's work."

"And you are confused?" His inquiry sounded condescending, his words jesting.

"Please do not laugh at me." Delight released an exasperated sigh. "Truthfully, the danger is not a blithe subject."

"Won't I face more peril as a part of the Continental army?"

"It appears so." How wrong she'd been in her evaluation of him, and it filled her with guilt.

He rested the lantern on the buckboard and grasped her shoulders. Peering into her face, he shook his head. "Ye can't rescue the whole world. Permit some of the rest of us to take on the responsibilities."

She didn't know where the tears came from, only that they flowed swiftly over her cheeks. "You are toying with me."

"Not at all, Lass. Ye desire this war to be ended, the British sent back across the Atlantic, no blood shed, and no one to suffer pain."

She nodded, unable to respond. Her musings were foolish.

"It's an impossibility," he continued. "James is a perfect example."

Swallowing hard, she managed to control her tears. "In some respects, I–I have never really grown up. For me to view our lives as a fairy tale is imprudent."

"Oh, ye are quite grown up, Delight." He gathered her into his arms. "Sometimes I think ye were robbed of your childhood with all your preoccupation in caring for others."

"My sisters say I'm domineering." She attempted a smile.

"That ye are." Henry met her smile. " 'Tis because ye love them and want their lives unfettered by life's problems."

How well you know me. It feels soothing and yet frightening. Oh, Lord, Thou knowest my stubbornness and my struggles to keep from being overbearing.

"Delight, what are ye thinking?"

"That you know me all too well."

"Aye, I have a reason, a very selfish one." Henry gathered her up in his arms, and she welcomed his embrace, yet perplexity over the future still reigned in her heart.

"What rules your motives?"

He caressed her cheek and slowly descended upon her lips. "The lovely woman in me arms, the one who has given me reason to wake each morning and dream about the future." He sealed his words with a feathery light kiss, then deepened it when she slipped her arms around his neck.

My dear Henry, I long to tell you how you have captured my heart, but I'm fearful. With the thought of your leaving in a few days and possibly not returning, I cannot muster the courage to tell you of my love.

When the sweet kiss ended, she found the strength to say but little. "I pray God guards you and keeps you safe."

"Thank ye," he whispered.

She sought release from his arms. Another moment, and she would reveal the insurmountable love building in her heart. For now, it was enough to relay her feelings in a kiss. Stepping back, she took a deep breath. "Perhaps we should see how Charity fares with James."

A frown crossed his face, and in the faint light of the lantern, his hair looked to be on fire.

"Are you angry with me?" she whispered.

Quickly a smile met her gaze. "How can I be? I'm overwhelming you, and I do apologize."

Must you read my thoughts so perfectly? If you do, then surely you know my innermost secrets.

"I want to look about the wagon a little more. If James awakens before I return, please summon me so I can find out where to make this delivery."

She took a few steps, not sure she wanted their time to end but insecure about their uncertain future: James's injury, Papa's absence, Henry's enlistment, and her inadequacies. A thought occurred to her, and she whirled around to find Henry watching her. "What else did Papa and you discuss about me?"

He offered a broad smile. "I am not at liberty to relay our every word, at least not at the present."

❧

Delight found Charity still holding James's hand. Her sister hadn't moved since she'd left her an hour earlier. Charity's tear-stained face glistened in the candlelight. No doubt, her every breath was a prayer.

Compassion overwhelmed Delight. *Oh, Lord, please touch James's body with Thy healing.*

His face looked placid yet pale, despite the stitched flesh beneath the bandages.

"Charity, I can sit with him now. Why don't you rest?"

She lifted her gaze and pressed her lips firmly together as though she hadn't heard a single word. Opening her mouth, she attempted to speak, but instead, she merely shook her head.

"You cannot nurse him back to health if you are exhausted," Delight whispered. When her sister failed to respond, she kneeled down and wrapped her arms around Charity's shoulders.

"I. . .need to be here in case he needs me."

"I understand." Delight touched their friend's forehead. Thankfully, he did not feel hot. "Praise God, no fever. Has he given any indication of awakening?"

"Not yet. Why don't you sleep?"

Delight smiled. "Do you honestly think I could with all this activity?"

Her sister offered a slight smile in response. "Not any more than I." Her frail shoulders sunk with a heavy sigh. "Where is Henry?"

"Tending to a few things in the barn."

"What did the barrels contain?"

"Gunpowder."

Charity gave no indication of surprise. "I thought as much. He has told me little about his business, but I suspected his endeavors were serious."

Delight braved forward. "Do you happen to know his destination?"

"Nay." She glanced into James's face and touched his cheek, as if his unconscious state allowed her such liberties. "We need to know soon, don't we?"

"Most assuredly." *Before good soldiers are killed for the lack of it.*

fifteen

Henry searched up and down the dark road for any signs of soldiers. He studied the brush and the slightest movement around him. Every shadow became suspicious, every sound a faceless man stealing across the night terrain. Bear remained inside and the house silent, yet Henry hesitated with every breath. Not only had someone attempted to kill his friend, but Henry also had the Butler household to consider. Evil men lay in wait somewhere.

How did James escape death and still keep the gunpowder intact? Why didn't the attackers steal the wagon while he lay in his weakened condition? Where and when did all of this occur? The questions ran repeatedly through Henry's mind, plaguing him like an army of rats. None of them could be answered until his friend gained consciousness.

Only when he decided to enter the house did he remember Delight's tender words. He knew without reservation she cared for him and not James. Although she did not convey her feelings with words, the truth glistened in her eyes and radiated from her face.

She had allowed him another kiss and responded shyly at first, then more fervently before pulling away. Delight Butler was not the type of woman to be frivolous with her affections, but he must proceed slowly.

Once he entered the hall, he watched the two sisters embrace. The sight warmed his heart as he recalled his own family left behind in Ireland. With a strange mix of awe, envy, and love, he realized the Butlers were his family now.

"You two can rest. I am here to keep a watchful eye on James," he said.

Delight laughed lightly. "I said similar words to Charity

upon my arrival, but she would not hear of it."

"Is that what ye are telling me?"

"Indeed," she replied. "Neither of us wants to relinquish one hour's sleep until we know James will be well."

"Aye, we are a strange threesome. . .but loyal ones." Henry studied James's face before easing down beside him. Deathly pale. *He does not look like he'll last the night.* From the corner of his eye, he saw Charity's tears. A selfish thread wove its way through his heart. In speaking his mind about his love for Delight, did he invite the same agony for her?

Henry waited through the night with Delight and Charity. They were all exhausted, but none would give in to more than a brief nodding off to sleep. James did not acquire a fever, surely a blessing, but the danger of infection had not yet passed.

Just before daybreak, Henry stood to stretch his legs. His friend's color looked better; hopefully it was not wishful thinking on his part, but a step toward healing.

"I should start breakfast," Delight whispered.

"And I should do the milking and the morning chores." He smiled into her weary face.

Charity brushed a wayward lock of dark hair from James's forehead. "I'm afraid to move for fear he will waken and no one will be here to tend to him."

"Then you must stay," Delight said

"But I shouldn't shirk my responsibilities," Charity said. "I always begin the preparations for the morning meal."

Delight patted her sister's arm. "I believe Remember or Patience will do quite well this morning without you. Here lies your responsibility."

"Mistress Butler will be disappointed in me, I am afraid," Henry said. "Neither of you rested during the night."

"Mama knew we would not adhere." Delight shrugged. "I'm sure of it."

"It appears that I am the only one who had sense enough to sleep." James spoke hoarsely and didn't open his eyes, but his humor broke the chill of the dismal night.

Charity instantly dropped his hand. "Oh, James, 'tis splendid to see you alive."

"Don't. . .you dare release my. . .my hand. Your touch kept me breathing." His words were slow and labored, but undoubtedly their lighthearted James was with them again.

Charity blushed scarlet but wrapped her fingers around his nevertheless.

"You gave us quite a scare." Delight sighed.

He forced a weak chuckle. "I scared myself, and I hurt in places I didn't know existed."

"You need your rest," Charity insisted. "Please, do not waste your strength by talking."

"First. . .first, I need to tell you about the wagon."

"I already found the contents," Henry said. "Corn, among other things. Where were you bound? That's all I want to know, so I can deliver it."

James closed his eyes. Excruciating pain passed over his features, and he drew in a shaky breath before continuing. "To Philadelphia. It is not much, but 'twill help. Thank. . ."

"Hush, James," Henry ordered. "Save yourself for healing."

He raised his hand, then dropped it. "A friend, Cavin Sullivan—" He swallowed hard and moistened his lips. "Was to meet me east of the city."

"No more, Friend, lest you do more damage to your old body than already has been done."

The injured man nodded and appeared to drift back to sleep.

Henry paced the floor. He wanted to take the wagon to Philadelphia, but he didn't know a Cavin Sullivan. The mystery of how he'd locate this man pounded at his brain. Asking the man's whereabouts once he arrived invited a wee bit of trouble. With a heavy sigh, he realized he needed to leave shortly, but he had not a destination. Perhaps a few hours' sleep was in order, or else he'd tumble to the ground while driving the wagon.

"I know Mr. Sullivan," Delight whispered. "He used to live in Boston."

"Could you describe him to me?"

She tilted her head. "He's Irish and has a thick mass of red hair."

"That describes me!" Suddenly Henry felt trapped with exasperation.

"Well, he's Papa's age and has a rounded middle." She glanced at Charity, then back to Henry. "He owns a tavern and drinks more than tolerable."

"Too many good men in this day and age drink too much." Henry shook his head, frustrated and not knowing which way to turn.

Delight smoothed her skirt. "I have no choice but to go with you."

"Absolutely not. I will not risk your life, nor will I go back on me word to Elijah."

"I promised Papa to watch your doings," Charity added.

"Did Papa speak to the entire family?" Delight's face reddened in anger, but her voice stayed low.

"Just Charity and me self," Henry replied.

Delight folded her hands in her lap. "Your promises make little difference, since I am the only one who knows Mr. Sullivan."

"Sister, consider the inappropriateness of traveling with Henry alone. It will be such a scandal."

"I must go. There's no other way."

Charity rubbed her cheeks, fatigue clearly written on her delicate features. "Then I will accompany you, for I couldn't live with myself if something happened to you."

"But what of James? You can't leave him unattended."

Her sister stared into James's face, then lifted her gaze to Henry. "Would you consider waiting one more day so I can be assured of his recovery?"

Oh, dear Lord, I promised Elijah to keep Delight safe and look after his family. Now, what am I to do?

"It is nearly two hundred and eighty miles to Philadelphia," Henry stated. "That is a good fourteen to fifteen days' travel with both of ye along."

"Are you saying you could make it in less time without us?" Delight raised a challenging brow.

"Precisely."

"Then we will make faster time with Charity and myself, for we both know how to drive a wagon."

"And pray tell, Lass, where do ye intend to sleep or even ride for that matter? Have ye forgotten the wagon bed is loaded with barrels?"

She touched a finger to her pretty wee chin, as he had seen her do so many times before. "We will all take turns driving, sharing a seat with the driver, and making do amongst the precious cargo."

"Delight Butler, ye are a stubborn one," he replied, wondering how Elijah ever got her to listen to reason.

"I'm not stubborn, but steadfast."

"Steadfast?"

"Being stubborn is a sin; steadfast is in the Scripture as an admirable trait."

He laughed despite his frustration.

"You give me no other choice." Charity pressed her lips tightly together. "I shall leave James's care to our sisters and ride along as a chaperon."

Henry thought he'd be ill.

੨੦

Delight slept with Charity curled beside her, since her sister refused to leave James's side. The extra day had strengthened him and given Charity peace of mind about his condition. Remember offered to tend to him, and Faith and Patience also offered their aid.

Henry, too, rested for the journey ahead. Due to the serious nature of the wagon's contents, they would be spending their nights under the wagon. A threesome, Henry had called them yesterday. Delight wasn't sure how she felt about the many miles that lay ahead. In one breath, she looked forward to his company, and in the next she feared the topic of their conversation. Love didn't choose who became tangled in its web; and for now, knowing Henry cared would help her through the war. In truth, she neither was ready for discussions about the future nor wanted them.

Her thoughts drifted back to Henry's kiss and his growing affections. Odd, she had thought of little else except him declaring his feelings; and now that he had, she quaked in her shoes.

Delight couldn't depend upon Charity to lead many discussions. She tended to shyness, although she did speak out earlier about the journey to Philadelphia—considerable gumption from a sister who whined and carried on about the slightest variance in her life. Charity obviously had matured into adulthood with a few new observations and surprises of her own.

As she considered the matter, Delight concluded that delivering several barrels of gunpowder while pursued by an unknown agent sounded considerably less risky than having Henry realize her immense love.

Moments before the departure, the three checked on James. He opened his eyes.

"You have a wonderful knack of waking at the most opportune moments." Charity bent to his side. "Henry, Delight, and I are leaving."

"For. . .where?" he managed to whisper. "Not Philadelphia?"

She nodded and offered a shy smile. "Aye, James. Delight knows Mr. Sullivan, and I am going along to chaperon."

James attempted to raise himself but could not lift his head. Charity gently eased him back onto the pillow. He blinked and cast his gaze around the room. "I see I'm in Henry's quarters."

"Right you are," Henry said. "But I shan't be needing them for a few days. How are you feeling?"

"Like somebody tried to kill me and nearly succeeded, but I survived their attempt."

"From the looks of you, surviving is debatable," Delight

said. "You need to rest. By the time we return, you will be riding bareback."

"Seriously," Henry began, "do ye feel well enough to state what happened? I am thinking I need to be prepared."

James nodded. "I suspected I was being followed about. . . ten miles out of Chesterfield."

"Take your time," Henry urged.

"Once dusk set in, I. . .left the wagon in a thicket and back-tracked. I came upon two men. . .on horseback—loyalists by the sound of 'em—who were bragging about what they were going to do to me."

James closed his eyes and took several deep breaths before resuming. "I surprised them. . .took their weapons, and tied them to a tree, but I wasn't expecting a third. He came from behind. We. . .struggled, and he knifed me before I got the utmost of him."

Delight cringed at what James implied. She knew better than to glance Charity's way, knowing her sister's weak stomach.

"I made it back to. . .to the wagon and set my sights on Chesterfield. Not sure how I got here. . .save by the grace of God."

"That is also why you're still alive," Charity said.

Little sister, you continue to amaze me, Delight thought.

"I know ye are in pain, but is there anything you can tell me about the men before we venture toward Philadelphia?" Henry asked.

James swallowed hard. "Two things you need to know. One. . .has been branded a thief. I saw a *T* burned into the flesh of his right hand. . .below his thumb. The other matter is the far barrel. . .on the left side of the wagon is filled with corn. . .just in case someone searches it."

"Thank you, Friend. I'll be heading outside while ye tell the women good-bye."

Delight had no intention of lingering behind. Charity and James deserved a few moments alone. "Farewell, James. I will be praying for your good health." She stood, then turned to her sister. "Charity, don't persist in tasking James's health. You will have ample time to visit when we return." She tossed a smile over her shoulder and hurried to the doorway behind Henry.

❧

Hours later, the wagon ambled on in a southwesterly direction. Plenty of food lay packed around the barrels, and true to Henry's assessment, both girls had a difficult time lying on the wagon bed. Sleeping would be done in an upright position. Thankfully, Mama had packed ample blankets for the cold nights and chilly days ahead. Delight refused to think of the explosion that could occur with a single musket blast in the right direction.

"What's in the barrels that is so important to the soldiers?" Mama had asked.

Delight decided to say nothing rather than lie to her mother.

"I took the lid off one and saw corn." Henry obviously skirted around the real topic.

Mama placed her hands on her hips. "Henry O'Neill, must I question you like Mercy and Hope—or Elijah?"

"Indeed, ye might, Mistress Butler." He leaned against the wagon, tugging at this and pulling at that.

"What is below the corn?"

"Ma'am, if there is anything beneath it, the Continental army has need of it."

Mama said nothing, only stared into Henry's face as the color rose up his neck in sharp contrast to his coppery red hair. "Perhaps I don't want to know what's in those barrels."

"A wise decision, Mistress Butler."

She wagged a finger at him. "You learned too many of Elijah's tricks while you two were together. Now you take good care of my girls, or I will skin you alive!"

"Of course. I would prefer a firing squad to facing you if something happened to one of them."

"Precisely. You'd best be leaving before I change my mind

about allowing them on this mission. I already feel I've lost my good senses by going along with this. . .trickery."

A few moments later, Henry took the first turn at driving, and Charity volunteered to sit among the barrels. Despite the uncomfortable position, she eventually slept, which in Delight's mind was impossible in the excitement.

She glanced up at the sky with its graying clouds. Although it could snow, she prayed it would wait until they returned. On the other hand, rain had a way of chilling one to the bone. "Do you think those two men will follow us?"

"Lass, they'd have to find us first."

She shivered. "My thoughts are they'd be very angry."

"And out for blood. Again, I say this venture is not for the fainthearted. I could still make arrangements to send ye and Charity back to Chesterfield."

She straightened on the seat despite the fact her back ached and walking looked more agreeable. "You are afraid of Papa?"

"And rightfully so. He once threatened to cut off my good leg if anything happened to one of his family."

"But my company is worth any risk."

He laughed heartily. "Are ye asking me to choose between my good leg and you?"

Teasing eased her heavy heart. " 'Tis a small price to pay for a lady's company, don't you agree?"

"Are ye worth the trouble?"

"Papa thinks so." *Do you, dear Henry?*

He nodded and pressed his lips together. "Me Delight thinks highly of herself. Pride cometh before destruction, Lass."

"A woman that feareth the Lord shall be praised."

Henry shifted his healing leg, and she sensed it stiffened. "I would like very much to drive now," Delight said. "Your leg needs a rest."

"I think not. It is fine," he replied. "Although we could quote Scripture all the way to Philadelphia to pass the hours."

"I am sure that would make Charity and Mama very happy. Remember is most likely praying for that very ideal."

"Why don't we recite the Song of Solomon?" His voice rang with laughter.

"Henry! What a shameful suggestion." *Those thoughts traverse through my mind enough without reminders*. She crossed her arms across her chest in feigned annoyance. "Perhaps I shan't speak to you at all until we return home."

"Then ye can listen, for I have much to discuss about us."

sixteen

Henry couldn't believe his daring, but he had experienced God's prompting to talk with Delight about their relationship. He sincerely doubted if she would jump from the wagon and walk home; she was far too committed to the patriot cause. And if she refused to listen, then obviously he'd misunderstood God's leading regarding their future together. His heart might be broken at the end of the journey and the rendezvous with Cavin Sullivan, but the Father had promised His abiding grace in times of adversity.

Delight perplexed Henry. She appeared to enjoy his conversation and they shared teasing readily, but her physical response to him fluctuated like the changing tides. She seemed to enjoy his embraces, then would pull away as if suddenly assaulted by guilt or remorse. . .or something. She might still have feelings for James, or perhaps she bore no strong feelings toward Henry other than friendship. In any event, he needed to have the answers.

"Delight, if not for this journey, I would be enlisting. I have no doubt that God placed me in your home for the purpose of understanding true liberty in Him and true freedom for men to govern themselves." He glanced at her pale face. Did his topic disturb her this greatly?

"I am pleased we were used for this noble purpose."

With only the sound of nature around them and the steady plop of the horses' hooves on the road, he continued. "Until I joined your family, I believed God intended the aristocrats to rule and the poorer classes to adhere to their mandates. I was convinced of this, even with the suffering of my own family in Ireland and the testimony of my friend Adam about his meager life in the slums of London."

"I'm sorry for all you have experienced." Her face looked earnest. "Previously the war felt like an adventure or a diversion, a topic to debate. I saw soldiers in British-occupied Boston, with all of their pomp and circumstance, arrest men and escort them away. I heard men and women shout of the unfairness and ministers speak against the British from the pulpit, but the situation angered rather than frightened me. Even when I carried messages in Boston—"

"Ye what?" Henry must have heard incorrectly.

She massaged her arms. "Papa did not tell you?"

"Tell me what?"

Delight moistened her lips. "I passed messages for the patriots while we lived in Boston."

Henry exhaled heavily into the chilly air. "I am not surprised, knowing your resolve in such matters. Did ye not consider the danger?"

"Not exactly. It exhilarated me. Of course, my illegal activities are why Papa moved us to Chesterfield."

"Wise man." *I wonder if I can handle the trouble involved in loving and marrying ye, Delight Butler.*

"As I was saying, that used to be my attitude. When you came, I saw the cruelty of war from a different perspective. I truly wanted to hate you, but I couldn't. As a result I was constantly angry. At times, I actually considered that there were good, Christian men in the British flanks, too. Now I realize you could have chosen to keep your views about the patriots to yourself, and our friendship might never have taken place." She cast him a sideways glance. "For selfish reasons, I am glad you are now a man of true liberty."

"I am delighted, too, Miss Delight."

She smiled before a wistful look passed over her face. "Papa's leaving awakened me to the atrocities involved in this struggle." She gazed into his face, her large eyes reflecting sadness. "Finding James in such a mangled, bloody condition did not help, either. Of course, you have seen more injured and fatally wounded men than you care to remember."

"True, and I will see it again."

She shuddered, and he did not think her reaction was due to the cold. She hesitated, then began again. "Forgive me, you were talking, and I should have been listening instead of voicing my own thoughts."

"Nonsense, I value ye words. Every comment helps me to know ye better. In addition, what I have to say involves your own thoughts and sentiments."

"Do continue, Henry. I won't interrupt."

Suddenly, all his carefully prepared statements escaped his mind. He didn't know why he'd initiated the conversation or what he planned to say. Stammering and feeling ridiculous, Henry chose to abandon the subject and try again another time—once he remembered what he wanted to tell her about his love and the future. Humiliation warmed him to the bone, and foolishness cast an accusing finger in his face.

An hour later he recalled the purpose of his initial discussion—the future—but courage failed him. He couldn't tell Delight he loved her or ask her to wait for him until the war ended. In all honesty, he wanted to marry her before he enlisted.

❧

Five days passed, five weary days that extended into the night. Delight endured the uncomfortable wagon and persisted through each hour with less and less sleep. Henry often refused her offers to drive, as well as Charity's. And he always waited until complete darkness before stopping for the evening.

The wagon held a heavy load, and despite the urgency, the animals required rest. Often Delight and Charity strolled alongside it; but in those rare moments when Henry allowed them to drive, he slept. His limp had all but disappeared; however, Delight noticed the way his leg stiffened after long periods in the wagon. She thought he must be exhausted, but he never complained.

Henry traversed away from settlements. No point in arousing suspicion about the barrels or having thieves steal their corn.

Sleeping under the wagon on cold, hard ground bruised her bones and threatened her disposition. Delight noted Charity grumbled not once, a rarity for her sister and an obvious improvement in her temperament. But of course, Delight herself had found patience in dealing with others of late. Perhaps both she and her sister were showing the signs of reaching maturity.

The past few days, Delight had wakened with a pounding headache that plagued her until nightfall. Stubbornly she refused to tell Charity or Henry, knowing they could do nothing about the growing pain. Her throat felt as though someone had sliced it raw. This was not the time to be ill, so she prayed.

Delight wondered time and time again what Henry had planned to say on the first day of their journey, but she hesitated to inquire. Deep down she understood his sincere feelings for her as readily as she knew her own. Something always held her back from initiating a conversation on the subject. Cowardice disgusted her, so she elected to term her reluctance to another cause, but what? She felt the pangs of fear every time she gazed into his blue eyes.

Several days out on their journey, the weather turned nippy. One morning they woke to a dusting of snow coating their blankets. Although it quickly melted, the threat of a heavy falling needled at her mind. Along with her other afflictions, she had noticed a slight cough. Delight concentrated on swallowing the annoyance so as not to alarm Henry or Charity.

By avoiding the more heavily traveled roads, they saw few people except during those occasions when they needed to gather directions. The three conversed freely as their journey lengthened. The topics covered everything from Henry's boyhood memories, his friend's recollections of London, Bible passages, and a mound of stories that Delight and Charity told of their childhood.

Delight loved Henry's teasing. His wit and charm increased her feelings for him. Talking with him reminded her of Papa, as though he sat in their midst instead of marching off to war. Many of Henry's admirable traits were the same characteristics she valued for a husband. Of course, considering him in the future sounded easier than approaching the subject at the present.

"Henry, do you sincerely intend to live in Chesterfield after the war?" Delight asked one late afternoon as the sun made its fiery descent and she rode in the wagon bed. "I know you have stated as such, but this country is vast."

"I believe so, Lass. In me heart, I want to settle down with a family and resume me weaving. Remember, it's why I purposed to come to this fair country."

She nodded. "I remember you telling me that very thing."

"Where do you plan to obtain this family?" Charity asked from the bench beside him.

Sister, do not force his reply. I'm not ready for this discussion—at least not now and certainly not in your presence.

Henry chuckled, a trait she had learned to recognize when he hesitated speaking about an uncomfortable issue. "It is all in God's providence. I believe I can provide for a family with my trade, but I do require a wife."

"And what are your requirements for a suitable spouse?" Charity continued.

Delight jabbed her finger into her sister's right side, but Charity ignored the touch.

"Are ye applying?" Henry's voice rang with merriment.

"Nay, but I thought I could recommend someone if I knew what you deemed important."

Henry urged the horses down the road. Soon they would need to stop for the night, and all of them wanted as many miles behind them as they could obtain. "A godly woman is essential. A woman with a sharp mind and who has convictions of her own appeals to me. Friendship is vital, and with that comes respect and admiration for each other."

"And what of beauty?"

Henry's laughter rang over the treetops. "Oh, Charity, I am not a comely man, so how can I ask God for loveliness in a wife? Although the idea does have merit."

"Henry, I think you are most dashing. Don't you, Delight?"

Charity, if we were at home, you and I would toss words like puppies tugging at a bone. In fact, I would tease you unmercifully in front of James until you begged for release.

"Don't you think Henry is handsome?" her sister repeated.

Delight fumed. Later she'd tell Charity to tend to her own matchmaking. "He is pleasing to look at, if one appreciates red hair."

"His hair is what distinguishes him from other men."

"It reminds me of a rooster's comb." Delight uttered the words before considering their content.

"Sister, dare you be unkind to our Henry?" Charity sounded appalled.

Properly chagrined, Delight sought to remedy the situation. "I didn't mean to be derogatory. The color is simply unusual."

Henry cleared his throat. "Ladies, I'd welcome it if ye could talk about matters other than me appearance."

"Certainly." Charity's honeyed words irked Delight. She glanced back at Delight and offered a sweet smile before turning her attention to the road. "Now, what were we discussing? Oh, now I remember, what Henry prefers in a wife."

"I completed my thoughts," he quickly interjected.

"Wonderful. Commendable, too. I have another challenge. This time it is Delight's turn."

Oh no!

"What do you desire in a husband?" Charity asked.

"Must we persist in this topic?" Delight envisioned her sister's neck as one of Mama's chickens in line for dinner.

"Aye. You are next, then I will give my desires."

Delight attempted to remember the items Henry had listed so she would not repeat them. If she did, she had no doubt that Charity would make pointed comments about the similarities. "Henry must surely be bored with this game."

"Nay, Lass. I am finding this portion enjoyable."

Trapped, she must endure her sister's folly. "A man who honors God above all things."

Silence.

"Nothing else, Delight?"

"Unselfish, loving, intelligent, capable of courage and strength."

Charity sighed. "Forgive me for my observation, but your description sounds like Henry."

You will be at my mercy this night, Delight promised her sister silently, then quickly added, "I believe I spoke in generalities. All Christian women want those qualities in a husband. This is the essence of a true gentleman."

"You are most insightful. And I do believe you are quite intelligent, Sister, with an apt mind and the qualities of a true friend. I only wish I had your beauty."

Red-faced, Delight chose not to respond. She'd lost in Charity's little amusement. Thankfully, dusk had replaced the light, for she could not look into Henry's face without sinking into a puddle of humiliation.

A few moments later she gathered her courage. "Charity, this is not the end of this matter."

"I certainly hope not. Such a pity for me to marry before you." Charity laughed until Henry joined in. At first Delight scrambled for the right words to express her anger, then she, too, broke into a fit of laughter. "Charity, I will get even," Delight said. "Then we will see who shares the mirth."

"I don't doubt your merciless spirit for an instant." Her sister giggled. "But it was such fun."

"Henry, are you going to allow this infraction into your private affairs without revenge?" Delight desperately attempted to disguise the smile on her face.

"Your sister is a worthy opponent. I am afraid King George's army has met their match. As for me, I am going to get some rest before morning arrives."

"I, too, shall sleep, but my mind will be spinning ways to defend my honor," Delight replied. *Sweet Charity, this deed will be avenged one day. If not by me, surely one of our sisters will catch you unaware.*

seventeen

Another day passed, and Henry still laughed over Charity's blatant questioning about what he looked for in a wife and what Delight sought in a husband. Now, as he hitched the team to the wagon with the cold whipping around his neck, he resolved to speak to his beloved before the sun set that day. By nightfall, he would know if he had a future wife.

Suddenly he heard a twig snap behind him. The skin on the back of his neck tingled. The sound couldn't be from the women. They had ventured in the opposite direction, and he would have heard their arrival. His gaze flew to his musket, lying across the wagon seat.

"Don't be considering a step near that gun," a voice said. "Just be standing there nice and quiet and don't be turning around."

An Irishman. "What can I do for ye?" Henry asked easily.

"Aye, answer a few questions, like what are ye doing with this wagon?"

Is this one of the men who attacked James? "I am transporting corn."

"Is it your own wagon?"

"It belongs to a friend." *James had said that one of the men who attacked him had a T branded into the fleshy portion of his thumb. I dare not anger this man for fear of endangering Delight and Charity.*

"Where is your friend?"

"He is nearly a week's ride from here. Why do ye ask?"

The musket barrel rested against his lower back. "I'm asking the questions. Me thinks this wagon is stolen. What do ye have to say about that?"

Henry wished he knew to which side of the war the man

held his allegiance. "As soon as I deliver the corn, I am returning his wagon."

"Your name?"

"Henry O'Neill."

"Do ye mind if I examine the contents of those barrels?"

"Corn is corn, Sir, but ye may look. The last one on the left is open."

"I well know!" the man responded. "Tell me what happened to the driver of this wagon before I send a musket ball into your back and spill your blood over this hard ground."

Henry needed to get the advantage of this situation before Delight and Charity returned. "I am not at liberty to say."

"Then ye will forfeit your pitiful life."

The gravity of the man's words settled like black smoke on the field of battle. "Dead men cannot provide information."

"Neither can they steal goods."

Henry searched for a weapon within his grasp. "I have not stolen anything. I am making a delivery of corn."

"Perhaps I haven't made me self clear."

From the sound of the man's voice, Henry realized he was about to draw his final breath. Meeting God face-to-face held indescribable merits, but his departure would leave Delight and Charity at the mercy of an unscrupulous man. He whirled about to shove the musket from the man's hands. It fired, piercing the air, piercing the violence of a man's soul.

As he struggled against the Irishman, Henry heard Delight scream. He'd attempt any feat to protect her and Charity—aye, shed the blood from his veins. The gun barrel slammed against the side of his head. Blinding pain spun him into anger. Blood trickled over his forehead and into his eyes, marring his vision.

"Stop! Please stop!" Delight's voice echoed around him. "Cavin Sullivan, he is one of us."

The man hesitated long enough for Henry to send a blow to the side of his face. He fell, and Henry sprawled on top of him.

"Stop! Henry, Cavin!" Delight pulled on his shoulders. "This is not the enemy."

Henry, no longer numb to her words, ceased his pounding and posed the question, "Are ye a patriot?"

"By all that's right and holy!" A purplish-blue bruise already colored the Irishman's cheek. "This is James Daniels's wagon!" He peered up. "Delight Butler, is it ye, Lass?"

"Aye, Mr. Sullivan."

"I have made a terrible mistake," Cavin sputtered.

Henry still felt rage surge through every part of him. He trembled and wiped the blood from his face and head with his arm. "Indeed, ye have."

Delight helped him to his feet while Charity assisted Mr. Sullivan. "James has been badly injured. We are transporting the barrels for him."

Cavin Sullivan gripped the side of the wagon and fought for his breath. "You throw a hard punch," he muttered.

"I don't take too kindly to a man sticking a gun in me back."

"I thought ye had stolen the wagon."

"Ye should've had the sense to ask." Henry found his temper rising again. *Help me, Lord, to gain control.* He drew in a ragged breath. "Tell the story while I calm me self."

The older man eyed him suspiciously. "James was late to our meeting place, and I went in search of him. I'd heard the story about a branded thief and two other loyalists searching for him and the wagon. I thought ye were one of them."

" 'Tis true. I'd have done the same thing." Henry's words appeared to soothe the man. "Hope I didn't hurt ye too much."

Mr. Sullivan offered a grim smile and stuck out his hand. "Glad to meet a good Irishman, even if I am on the opposite end of his fist. I imagine your head is a wee bit throbbin'."

"Indeed it is." The man's missing front tooth told Henry that he held the infamous Irish temper. He extended his hand and the two shook. "Whereabouts ye from?"

"Near Dublin. And ye?"

"County of Londonderry, province of Ulster."

Delight handed Henry a wet cloth, and Charity did the same for Mr. Sullivan. "Ye lasses are a gift from God," the older man said. "Ye certainly saved two Irishmen from killing each other." He wiped his bruised face and turned to Delight. "I see ye are still aiding the patriots. And what of Elijah?"

"He enlisted."

The Irishman's eyes sparkled. "Couldn't stop that man."

A twinge of jealousy about the man's familiarity with Delight pulled at Henry, but he refused to let it show. *Forgive me, Lord. Ye hast given me a new friend, and I am behaving shamefully.* "How can we help ye?"

"Oh, 'tis me to lend a hand. I have a wagon back in the woods to carry the barrels. I will take them on to Philadelphia."

"Praises to God," Henry replied. "I'll help you load, then we can journey back to Chesterfield." He studied his recent opponent's face. "You might need a bit of rest and nourishment before setting out alone."

"I brought a bit of rum—" He stopped and cringed. "Pardon me, lasses, I know how your father feels about the spirits, but it does numb the pain."

"And your mind to clear thinking. Our Lord taught us about the dangers of drunkenness," Delight said with a lift of her chin.

That's my sweet Delight. She never hesitates to tell one the truth—except when it comes to her heart.

❧

The road home. The words alone sounded like manna to Delight. Weariness tugged at her whole being. She had offered to sit on the wagon bed; and with the extra room available now that the barrels had been unloaded, she lay down and instantly fell asleep. Strange and terrifying dreams plagued her, so strange she believed she was awake only to realize otherwise.

"Delight. Delight."

She knew Charity shook her, but she couldn't awaken. Her head pounded like a soldier's drum. "Let me sleep. I am so tired."

Am I dreaming again or is Charity still talking?

"Henry, her head is so hot. We must do something."

Delight's thoughts drifted back to a dream where Papa and Henry rode down the road toward their house in Chesterfield shouting, "The war is over! The British are defeated!" A hand touched her forehead, then caressed her cheek. It did not belong to Charity.

"Delight, can ye answer me?" His voice rang tender to her ears.

She attempted to stir and reply, but her throat felt as though a hot poker had seared it. The words failed to form. Only the semblance of a moan met her ears. Blissful sleep caught her like the waves that used to slap against Boston Harbor, and she felt herself sweeping out to sea.

৯

Henry had realized helplessness in his days, but nothing like the overwhelming despair of watching Delight suffer with fever and delirium. She fought the blankets Charity tucked in around her, while a swirl of new-fallen snow quietly covered her body.

"We need shelter." He urged the horses down the road. "I remember a village a few miles ahead. We will seek a place to stay and medicine for Delight."

Charity sat at her sister's side, continually dabbing her flushed face. "Perhaps we can find some broth and a warm place for her to sleep. I care not for myself, but this fever must be broken."

Henry ached at the thought of his beloved's illness. "I should never have allowed ye to come. Being exposed to the elements has made Delight ill, and ye may possibly be next."

"Nonsense, I feel perfectly fine. The truth be known, I noticed Delight had a slight cough before we met up with Mr. Sullivan."

Henry tightened his hold on the reins. "Why didn't she say something?"

"Delight? She never admits to feeling poorly for fear someone else may need tending."

"I understand exactly what ye are describing. At times she

reminds me of a hen fussing over her chicks, the way she treats ye and your sisters." The longer he considered the matter, the more irritated he grew with himself. "It's time she allowed someone to take care of her."

"That will take a few hundred prayers."

"I have another idea." Henry glanced up at an angry sky. It matched his mood. If they did not find a hospitable home, they would be covered in snow. Delight desperately needed a roof over her head.

"So do I," Charity replied. "Marry her, and none of us will have to fret over whether she is taken care of properly."

"Aye." His voice saddened. "I would most gladly oblige, but I fear she doesn't hold the same affections as I do."

"Henry O'Neill. How can you be so clever and still not understand what Delight feels for you?"

Curiosity mixed with frustration assaulted him. "She's had opportunities to reveal more of her feelings but has chosen not to. I know she cares for me, but is it enough to withstand the future?"

"Love does peculiar things to a woman," Charity said. "You may want that very thing until you find it, then you are afraid. Has she welcomed tenderness in one breath and shied from it in another?"

"You know 'tis true. What can I do?"

Snow began to trickle down in huge flakes. "Make her think exposing her heart is her idea. She's too stubborn to do so otherwise. For the present. . ." Charity faltered. "We must pray, for her fever is rising."

Henry caught his breath and glanced behind him where Charity held a blanket over Delight's face to keep the wind and snow away. "Does she have a rash or is her breathing irregular?"

"Nay. For that we must be grateful."

"Father God," Henry began, "I know I have been amiss in allowing Delight and Charity to join me on this ominous journey, and I am truly sorry. But it seems my errant ways have contributed to Delight's illness. Please touch her with Your healing power and break the fever raging through her body. In Your holy Son's name, amen."

He looked ahead into a swirling mass of white and saw the outline of a house and barn. *Thank Thee, Father. May these people be good Christian folk.* "I see help ahead."

Within minutes, Henry pulled the horses to a halt and braked the wagon. He stepped down onto his bad leg, and it nearly collapsed. Righting himself, he faced a snarling dog that had no intentions of allowing him to pass.

"What do you want?" a male voice called from the door.

The dog stepped closer. "Shelter and possibly broth for an ill woman in my wagon. I can pay."

"Ill, ya say?" the man asked in a raspy tone.

Henry couldn't turn to face him for fear the dog would sink his teeth into his uninjured leg. "Yes, Sir. She has a fever."

"Is it pox? We don't want any sickness here."

Henry had feared the same thing. He knew well the deadly effects of smallpox. "She does not have a rash. I believe it's from exposure to the weather; we have been traveling awhile."

The dog growled. "Can you call off your dog?"

"Not until I'm ready. Besides, my wife and I don't want sickness at our door."

Obviously you aren't generous in spirit. Henry cringed and clenched his fists. "Perhaps some broth then?"

"I will ask the wife, but you cannot come inside."

Henry glanced at the barn. "May we rest in your barn?"

The man said nothing, and since Henry couldn't see him, he waited. "I'll pay for the use of it."

Silence echoed around the wagon.

"All right, you can use the barn. Don't want no money except for hay, and you can feed my animals while you are taking up room."

Is there no end to his rudeness? "I agree, Sir. Now will ye call the dog?"

"King George come here, I say." The mangy animal skirted

around the front of the wagon. Henry whirled around and saw it leap onto the porch beside the old man, who closely resembled the dog. "I'll ask my wife if there is food inside, but I can't promise anything."

"Thank ye. Any herbs for tea would be appreciated."

"You keep asking for more! And don't be starting a fire or coming outside when it is dark. The dog guards things real well."

eighteen

Henry carried Delight inside the barn and placed her on a makeshift mattress of hay covered with a blanket. Once the door closed, the draft vanished. Still she needed to be kept warm—Charity, too. In this structure, they had little more than shelter, and all he could offer Charity to eat was soldiers' provisions of hard biscuits and dried beef, unless the farmer and his wife found food to spare. At least they had a lantern.

The owner did not complain when Henry led the horses inside. "I'll be expecting good payment for the hay," he'd shouted.

Oh, me Delight. I never wanted this for ye. But I will get warm food for ye and Charity and herbs no matter what the cost. He would wait a moment more before he ventured outside to the house and faced the nasty temperament of the owner and his mongrel.

King George! What a fitting name.

With twilight fast approaching, Henry looked for a tool to keep distance between him and the dog. Oddly enough, the barn was well maintained and neat. Various tools hung on pegs or leaned against a wall according to size. He had expected the contents to be in disarray to match the old man's disposition. Snatching up a hoe, he headed for the door.

"Henry, do be careful." Charity wrapped a spare blanket around her shoulders.

"I will, Lass. No matter what ye hear, stay put. I have a feeling the dog and I might have a skirmish." He grinned for her sake. "Pray the man's wife is friendlier than he."

She nodded. Her obligatory smile soon faded when Delight moaned.

Without another word, Henry slid open the barn door. As

145

expected, the dog approached him in a fury.

"King George, get out of me way." Henry raised the hoe. "I aim to converse with those people, and the likes of ye will not stop me."

The door of the house opened, and the old man stepped out, his hand grasping a musket.

"What are you doing with my hoe?"

Henry kept one eye on the dog and shouted back, "I'm protecting me self from your dog. I need to purchase warm food for the women and possibly something for fever."

"I heard you before," the old man said.

From behind him, a plump woman with snow-white hair pushed by the old man. "King George, get into the house this minute!"

Immediately the dog obeyed.

"The lady is ill?" she asked, moving toward Henry. "And you need food and herbs for a fever?"

"Aye, Ma'am."

"Rachel, you don't know what that woman has. Could be we might get sick and die," the old man spat.

"I am already old and ready to meet my Maker, Horace, and I intend to help." She neared Henry and smiled. "I'm Rachel Henderson. You bring those women inside. I have beef stew and medicine to help break the fever."

Thanks be to God.

Henry refused to sleep that night. He sat by Delight's side near the fireplace just as she had done for him. Charity stretched out on the other side of Delight, finally succumbing to sleep. The Hendersons were hospitable after all, simply cautious about loyalists, although the dog's temperament could not be disguised. Mistress Henderson had brewed some feverfew tea, and Henry had helped Charity administer it. Now he waited and prayed.

Mistress Henderson declared herself a believer, but her husband had no use for God. Henry could not imagine the misery of people who did not know Jesus as their Savior. How wretched they must feel with the uncertainty of life. It was difficult enough to face sickness, death, and the struggle to survive during these war-torn days, but to have no hope must be the epitome of despair.

Delight's face tinted pink with the fever looked peaceful, but the color veiled her ill health. Her lips, normally a deep wine, were now purple. He bent and brushed a kiss across her forehead.

"Me sweet lady," he whispered. "I pray the fever breaks tonight with God's healing. I want to see the light in your eyes, the sparkle that reminds me of heaven's gate. I love ye, Delight, with an affection I never thought possible."

Henry continued to watch her, wiping her forehead with a cool, damp cloth and praying. She was strong and healthy; she could recover in a few days with rest and proper food. His mind wandered back to special moments with her. Even their initial quarreling reigned as cherished moments. A strong woman, his Delight. Psalm 37:4 rang through his mind, as it had done so many times before: *"Delight thyself also in the Lord; and he shall give thee the desires of thine heart."*

Aye, I'm sure the Lord is pleased with ye. Always I see ye strive to serve Him. What a worthy mother ye will make someday. I pray He allows ye to be the mother of our children.

⁂

Shortly after midnight, Henry added another log to the fire and studied Delight's face. No longer did color tinge her cheeks and perspiration bead upon her forehead. Elated, he touched her cheek. Coolness met his fingertips.

"Praise God," he whispered. He stared into her lovely features. "Charity, wake up. The fever's broken."

Immediately Delight's sister sat upright and confirmed Henry's words. "It is a blessing," she whispered, "a real blessing."

Delight opened her eyes and glanced about, obviously confused by her whereabouts.

"We're in a farmhouse, Lass," he said. "How are ye feeling?"

She took a deep breath. "I was having the most beautiful dream, then voices woke me." She attempted a smile. "I gather I've been ill."

"Not for too long," Henry reported. "But long enough to cause us a scare."

"Forgive me." She swallowed with difficulty. "My throat aches, and I have a horrible taste in my mouth."

"The taste is the herbs," Charity said. "And tea will help soothe the pain in your throat."

Delight stared into Henry's face with a tender smile. "Someday I'll tell you about my dream. . . . For now, I'd like to sleep."

ॐ

Two days later, Henry, Charity, and Delight climbed into the wagon and said good-bye to Rachel and Horace Henderson. Henry wanted Delight to rest another day, but she insisted on traveling home.

"I can rest in the back of the wagon as easily as I can here," she argued. Nothing could convince her otherwise, and she used her stubborn nature to its fullest.

Rachel hugged her tightly. "I pray you will be stronger than ever before."

Delight felt tears well up in her eyes. "Thank you, thank you for everything you have done."

"It was a true blessing," the old woman answered. She leaned to whisper in Delight's ear. "Henry is a good man. You might consider marriage; he is quite devoted."

"I promise."

The wagon wheels crunched into a fairly heavy coating of snow as the horses ambled down the road. The whitewashed countryside and ice-laden trees painted an air of serenity against the stark blue sky. If the weather stayed crisp and not bitter cold, they could very well be home before the next snowfall. Delight felt exhilarated, ignoring her weakened condition and a dull headache that plagued her like a pesky fly in the heat of August.

Gratefulness to be alive soared through her veins, or did her renewed spirit extend from her love for Henry? In any event, she was eager to resume their journey home. Yet in the same breath, she knew home also represented the growing nearness of Henry's departure. Sadness descended upon her. She refused to think of life without him. She would cling to the memory of her fevered dreams.

In them, she and Henry had a home of their own in a rolling countryside filled with green pastures and pastel wild-flowers. The two walked through the fields hand in hand while in the distance children squealed with laughter and called to "Mama" and "Papa." What a lovely, sweet dream. She and Henry, a part of God's divine plan.

"Horace shook me hand," Henry remarked, glancing back at her with a smile wider than the Atlantic.

"Did he say any parting words?" Charity asked.

"Only to stop for a visit if we were in this area again."

Charity shook her head. "Delight, his treatment of us when we first arrived was appalling. And I thought King George would tear Henry to pieces."

"Glad I slept through it, but I am so sorry you two were exposed to his bad manners and his monster dog on my account."

"I'd do it again." Henry lifted the reins and coaxed the horses a little faster down the road.

"Why is that?" Charity asked in her familiar lilt.

Charity, will you ever cease wrapping every statement you utter around Henry and me?

He chuckled. "My good leg of course! I don't want to face Elijah and Mistress Butler's wrath."

They shared a good bit of teasing all morning long. The weather warmed, and the snow melted. Deer bounded across the road, their grace and spirit reminding Delight of Mercy and Hope at play. She missed her sisters and wanted to be home. There was no doubt that only the push of God would cause her to endeavor a lengthy wagon journey again. She felt a burst of energy.

"I am strong enough to drive," Delight announced the second morning after leaving the Hendersons. With the provisions Rachel had given them, they'd had a filling breakfast and felt an eagerness to put miles behind them.

"I think not," Henry replied. "When ye drove before your illness, ye hit so many ruts I feared the gunpowder would explode."

"I believe Charity drove then."

Charity tossed her a knowing look. "You are mistaken, Delight. I remember how I attempted to sleep between the barrels and realized I had either broken all my bones or my body was permanently bruised."

Delight did not recall their reporting the incidents quite the same way at the time, but it made for lively conversation. Anything to keep her mind diverted from the nearness of the moment when Henry would leave for the war. In the deep recesses of her mind, while she battled the fever, she thought he'd sat by her side and told her of his love. She sought to mention it to Charity and inquire as to the authenticity of her memory. The risk of appearing foolish always stopped her. During the time of the fever, she had experienced difficulty differentiating between her dreams and what truly happened, although her sister would not make light of it at all.

"Nevertheless, I'm so tired of this wagon. Can I please ride on the bench for awhile?"

Charity wiggled her shoulders, and Delight knew she had conjured the perfect reply. "Henry, do you mind if I drive?" She whirled around to her sister. "Do forgive me, I misunderstood. You must want to ride beside Henry, not me."

When we are home again, I will not be revengeful, Delight thought, *but I will find ways to torment you out of love.* "Charity, you plague me worse than a nest of angry bees."

"I learned well from my older sister. Henry, I do hope you don't mind. Delight wants to be near you for a change of landscape."

Most assuredly you speak the truth; but Charity, please, you do not have to inform him of the matter.

Henry brought the horses to a halt. He helped Charity into the wagon bed and extended his assistance to Delight. As soon as his fingers touched hers and grasped her hand, she caught the familiar tenderness in his gaze and the smile he offered only to her. Suddenly the first and then the second time he kissed her danced across her mind, leaving her weak in the knees and trembling to the touch.

"Aye, Lass, ye are still not well. I feel ye trembling." His hands seized her waist and lifted her to the wagon bench.

"Nonsense, I am quite strong."

Once they were on the road again, she did note her spirit felt exhilarated at sitting next to him.

"Do you think we could discuss a few important matters?" he asked quietly.

How can we with Charity straining to hear every whisper? She stole a glance and saw he peered down the road as if concentrating on every melting flake of snow. "Of course. Before you begin, I am most grateful for your kind care during my illness."

"Ye are most welcome, Lass. Charity's and your safekeeping had been entrusted to me, and I gave me word to your parents."

Did his voice crack or was it her imagination? "What are the pressing matters you speak of?"

He sighed. "I believe you already know." He glanced at Charity, and she slid to the back of the wagon and allowed her feet to dangle over the side.

Thank you, Sister. This may be our only opportunity to. . .to converse about private matters. Delight clasped her hands in an effort to hide her nervousness. "Continue, Henry."

From the corner of her eye, she saw his chest and shoulders rise with a deep breath. "I've thought about this at great length." His gaze swung to her. "Do. . .do ye have affections for me that are strong enough to last. . .until the Lord calls us home?"

nineteen

The illumination in Henry's eyes must have marveled the gates of heaven. Delight had dreamed, even seen a glimpse of that special radiance, but this brilliance far surpassed her deepest wishes.

"Do you not know?" she managed through a ragged breath.

"I've hoped and prayed," he replied in the same softness.

"I care for you. I care very much." Her heart beat fiercely. Her stomach fluttered as though a myriad of butterflies had suddenly taken flight.

"Dare it be love?" His face grew ghastly pale; he dragged his tongue over his lips. "Delight, I do love ye."

A small cry escaped her lips, and her eyes filled with joyous tears. "And I love you."

He pulled in the reins and set the brake. His hands shook so he could barely complete the task. In the next instant he drew her into his arms. "It seems I've waited a lifetime to hear ye repeat those words—words sweeter than honey."

She lifted her face to meet his, silently begging for a kiss to seal the love bubbling inside her. He did not disappoint. Henry's lips claimed hers lightly; but with the fervency of the moment, the kiss deepened, and she eagerly responded. Her hands reached for his neck, and she raked her fingers through the mass of copper-colored hair.

He finally pulled himself from her. "Thank ye for letting me speak me heart."

Delight knew she had to be completely honest. "I am afraid, Henry. I'm fearful of the war and of your not returning. I could not bear living without you."

He touched his finger to her cheek. "I know, me Delight. But God has a span of time for each of us. He's marked our days, and there is nothing we can do to alter His plan. I promise I will do what is noble and right for our country and, God willing, return to you."

Oh, Father, this apprehension of mine has kept me from loving Henry totally in my heart. Guard him, I beg of Thee. "I sense my trust in God faltering each time I think of you. I am so sorry."

He offered a slight smile. "I've read it in your eyes, and I will continue to pray for our Father's peace."

"Are you two finished with all your whisperings?" Charity called from the rear of the wagon.

Startled, Delight realized she had momentarily forgotten her sister's presence. "Probably not," she answered with a laugh.

"From the lack of conversation, I am assuming you two are engaged once more in a kiss," Charity continued. "I refuse to look for fear I might be embarrassed."

"Most assuredly." Henry chuckled. He took Delight's hand into his and kissed it.

"Papa and Mama will hear of this." Charity giggled. "After all, I am the chaperon."

"I shall be the first to tell." Henry's familiar wide smile broke across his rugged features. "In fact, I will shout it to all the world." He winked at Delight. "I love Delight Butler," he shouted. "I love the most fair lass in the whole world, and she loves me!"

Hours later they still chatted away, their conversation floating from one topic to another, but always with enthusiasm.

"When we have some privacy, I will ask ye to marry me," Henry whispered.

"And what if I should ask you?" Delight tingled from head to toe from his attentions. She attempted to look serious, yet a smile tugged at the corners of her mouth.

"Oh, ye are a modern lass," he replied. "Shall I beware of finding us alone?"

"You two are properly suited," Charity called from the

wagon bed. "I can recall a time not so long ago when you loathed each other."

" 'Twas a mere disguise of love," Henry said.

"I think you should wed the same day we return to Chester-field," her sister announced.

Delight felt her heart slam against her chest. As elated as she felt, a wedding could not take place until the war had ended. She refused to be a widow. Nay, they should wait until peace blanketed the land. Lifting her gaze, she saw Henry studying her curiously.

Henry, do not take Charity seriously. It is. . .impossible.
"We cannot wed until after the war," she said softly.

A grim sadness captured her. In a moment, his happiness seemed to vanish. *I've hurt him, but surely he can see how foolhardy it would be to do otherwise.*

෨

Henry kept both hands on the reins and gripped them hard. Masking this disappointment was one of the hardest feats he'd ever attempted. Like a giddy young man, he had assumed Delight felt the same commitment as he and would marry him this very day if possible, but her vision of marriage lay in the future. The thought pained him greatly, and he fought hard to recover his former enthusiasm.

I'm being selfish. If I were killed, she'd be a widow. I don't want a lonely life for her.

"Of course, that would be utmost, Lass. We can have a wonderful wedding with all of your family after the war."

"Splendid." She snuggled close to him and linked her arm in his. "For a moment, I feared you to be unhappy with me."

"The war could last a very long time. Perhaps another year," Charity called from the back.

Even longer, and every day would be miserable without my beloved to come home to. I'd agree to anything to keep her.

Delight abruptly straightened. "Surely not, Sister. With the British defeated at the Battle of Saratoga, we must be facing mere months."

"What do you think, Henry?" Charity asked. "Could you and Papa be home in so short a time?"

He carefully formed his words, not wanting to dishearten the women but believing there were many battles yet to fight before the British granted freedom to America. "Lasses, Saratoga is in New York. What of the South? Thirteen colonies exist where other British and American soldiers will battle. General Washington has a grand plan, I am sure, but things of this nature take time."

Silence echoed around him. Guilt assailed him for forcing reality into their tender hearts. "I did not mean to upset you," he finally said.

"You spoke the truth," Charity said. "James, with all of his zeal and enthusiasm, says the same."

"I do not agree with you!" Delight slung the words as though pitching soiled straw from a barn. "We may not have fancy uniforms or generals of nobility, but we have the cloak of truth."

"Truth is certain," Henry agreed, "but the cause takes time, effort—and the blood of men to lead it to victory."

Defiance etched her face. "Perhaps you do not truly harbor freedom and liberty in your soul."

"And perhaps ye do not really know me at all."

&

Four days more, and the wagon rumbled over the outskirts of Chesterfield. Delight no longer felt exhilarated in the return, for she and Henry had not spoken since their disagreement. Anything she wished to convey to him was spoken through Charity; and to her frustration, Henry acted as though nothing uncomfortable existed between them. Delight knew her childish behavior needed to stop, but her pride interfered. She wanted to apologize sincerely, but the words refused to come.

When she looked back on it, she realized she'd hurt him twice: first in her refusal to marry him before he enlisted and second in questioning his allegiance. Charity had scolded her severely, then hugged her and told her she loved her. Her sister was disappointed, Henry distressed; and Delight shouldered all the blame.

Why can't I simply say I was wrong? Have I not learned anything from Scripture?

A horrible thought sickened her. What if Henry should be hurt or killed in the days ahead, and she had not mended the problem between them? What if he became so disillusioned with her argumentative spirit that he found another woman to ease his wounded heart? She resolved to wait not a moment longer. Already the last house in Chesterfield came into view. From there, they would soon reach home, and from there would come his enlistment.

"Henry," she said meekly from the back of the wagon.

"Aye." His tone balanced between cordial and impersonal.

"I want to say—"

Charity gasped. "Are those British soldiers in the distance?"

He pulled the wagon to a halt. "Lass, I believe ye are right."

Delight rose to her feet as the sum of her nightmares came within her view. Redcoated uniforms glittered in the afternoon sun, reminding her of blood shed for the cause of liberty. "Henry, you must run before they find you."

Charity grabbed the reins from him. "Yes, don't let them see you."

He whirled his gaze to Delight, his look filled with the love he had hidden for the past four days.

"Please, go." Delight reached to touch his shoulder, but the horses took a step and jolted the wagon. He steadied her, his touch scorching her flesh.

"Go with him," Charity said. "Now, before they see how many of us are in the wagon. I can take care of myself."

Delight needed no more urging and swung her leg over the side while Henry jumped to the ground. Grabbing his musket, Henry grasped Delight's hand, and the two raced toward the woods. She wondered about his injured leg, but for the present it didn't slow him.

God help us!

"Do you see them?" she asked breathlessly, afraid to peer behind. One hand clung to Henry's, and the other held her skirts. Desperation and fear riddled her senses.

"Nay, but they will surely inquire of Charity. I believe they are looking for me."

Alarm seized her. "Will they harm her?" They raced into thick underbrush, where she stopped to gain her breath. Henry studied the wagon and soldiers.

"I think not. They have no reason to suspect anything amiss." He hesitated. "She has just met up with them."

Delight scurried to view the scene. "I am sorely worried about her."

"Do not worry about your sister. She is stronger than she appears."

A remembrance of the past weeks danced across her mind. Charity had amazed her on more than one occasion with her cleverness and gumption. "I comprehend what you are saying. I've seen and felt an inner strength that I greatly admire."

He sighed. "I don't like the fact that she is the one who must endure the soldiers' questioning. At the moment, selfishness is creeping all over me. I shouldn't have left her alone, fleeing like a scared boy."

"If you had stayed, you would be on your way back to fighting for the wrong side."

He nodded and continued to study the British, who had turned their horses around and trailed after Charity and the wagon.

Another stab of alarm snatched at her heart. "Why do you suppose they are following her?"

Henry stared at the small parade as though he were reluctant to speak his mind. "Possibly Abby Rutherford is hosting them for tea."

She heard the bitterness in his voice. "Are you thinking she may have alerted them to your whereabouts?"

"And those of James."

Oh, no, poor Charity. "They would not be kind to him, would they?"

"Nay, Lass. If they have him, he faces serious trouble."

"What shall we do?"

He turned and offered a smile. "Always we. Must you continually become involved with the perilous aspects of life?"

His infectious grin subdued her irritation. How many times had she asked herself the same question? "I know I am independent."

"But are ye totally dependent on God?"

Henry's inquiry burned to the core of her being. *How could he ask such a despicable thing, especially at a time like this?* "Of course I am."

"Are you, Delight? Completely? Without hesitation?"

An inner voice stirred her being. *Could Henry be correct in his assessment?*

I don't think so. I am the oldest; it is my nature to look after others.

But in doing so, are you trusting Me?

Delight trembled. The truth assaulted her. She did trust more in herself than in the Creator. Oh, she prayed, but too many times when circumstances required immediate attention, she acted before relying on God. Deep down, she knew He didn't need her assistance. God simply asked for her loving obedience.

She blinked and stared up at Henry, feeling his gaze upon her. He showed no condemnation, only an earnest desire for her to respond to his concerns.

Perhaps my weakness has changed his heart for me. Even worse, perhaps God may no longer feel I'm worthy of His favor.

Again the inner voice pricked her spirit. *I will never leave thee, nor forsake thee.*

Oh, Father, I am so sorry. Please forgive me and lead me in the right paths.

A tear slid down her cheek, and she shook her head to dispel the host of emotions flowing through her: remorse, regret, guilt. She prayed God's incredible love would ease the pain she had caused.

"What is it, Darlin'?" Henry brushed the tear from her face. "I didn't mean to inflict the pain I see in your eyes. I had no right to ask ye about your own relationship with the Lord."

She swallowed her tumultuous mental anguish, wanting to speak clearly. "But you had every right, for I know your inquiry arose from love for me. I am sorry for what I said to you earlier. I–I despise my stubborn nature. Far too often, I believe I have the correct answers and must be in control of my destiny."

His demeanor softened, revealing a contrite man. "Me Delight, ye are in the presence of a self-righteous man. God must forever be humbling me."

She paused, wondering how much she could speak her mind without risking Henry's possible rejection.

Go ahead, My child. Tell him your heart.

"I want to be your wife," she whispered. "I was afraid before. I thought if I lost you in the war, it wouldn't hurt as badly. I despise my harsh words; they were all lies. Please forgive me."

He opened his mouth, but she covered it with her fingertips. "You are so good and kind to me, more than I deserve. Aye, perhaps a little self-righteous at times." She smiled and bit her lip to keep from weeping. "But, if you will have me, I will marry you this very hour."

He gathered up the fingers caressing his lips and kissed them lightly. "I accept your humble proposal." He slipped his hand around her waist to the small of her back and drew her close. "I love your free spirit, and I love your determination. With God's help, we will have a beautiful life together. Ye are my delight from the Lord. With ye beside me, God has given me the desires of me heart."

She whisked away a tear. "But I can be bitter and relentless."

"Aye, so can I, but we are sweet as honey together." His lips were but a hair span from hers, and in the next instant he sealed his words. When at last he pulled from her, he held her close, so close she could hear his heartbeat. He released a heavy sigh. "Indeed I'm a self-centered man, basking in the presence of my beloved when Charity and James may be in grave danger."

"What are you going to do?" She carefully chose her words to separate herself from the solution.

He smiled and kissed the top of her head. "I think we should move around the trees and the town to your home. Once everything looks clear and dusk has set in, I will send ye to your mother so she can see ye are well and safe."

"And James?"

"Let us pray he is in seclusion and that God will protect him."

Hand in hand, they moved just inside the thicket of trees, wary of the sights and sounds around them and coaxing the sun to set. Speaking in whispers and only when necessary, they edged around Chesterfield, ever mindful of the soldiers in their red coats. From all appearances, the British looked to search every house in the small town.

"Are ye praying?" Henry asked as they watched soldiers dismount at a home across the way from Uncle Matthew and Aunt Anne's whitewashed two-story.

"With all my might."

"I wish I could do something instead of observe. This is a helpless feeling."

"What is God telling you?"

He squeezed her hand. "He is in control. I believe I'm proceeding as He desires."

twenty

Twilight painted the sky in colors of rich amber fading into deep blue. Another day finished, yet tasks haunted Henry with their lack of completion. Delight and he rested beneath a knoll on the hard, cold ground while waiting for darkness to completely settle. Twice they had observed soldiers coming and going at the Butler household. Neither time did the redcoats bring anyone out, leading Henry to believe James had secured safety. Charity either remained in the home or had fled with him. He preferred the latter possibility, since his friend had received serious injuries and could not yet be fully recovered.

He glanced at Delight, her face etched with exhaustion and her recent recovery from the fever. She needed to be sitting beside a warm fire and out of the cold air before she fell prey to the illness again. He wrapped his arms around her in hopes of keeping her warm.

Oh, Father God, please heal those around me who are fighting disease and injury. Give us all strength and courage in these difficult times.

"I'd like for you to enter your home from the front," he said, hating to be apart from her but knowing her health came foremost. "I doubt if the soldiers plan to return this evening."

She snuggled into the hollow of his shoulder. "I would rather be here with you, but those inside might need a helping hand. And certainly Mama and Charity share worrisome thoughts about us." She did not say a word about his possible imprisonment if captured, and neither did he. "Charity may need comfort, too."

"Quite possibly. If I will not endanger your family or James with my presence, pass a candle three times at the rear. I'll

161

arrive shortly. If there is trouble—"

"There shan't be." She rose from her crouched position and massaged the small of her back.

Henry tugged on her arm, pulling her back down beside him. He stole a kiss, then grinned. "So ye won't forget me."

"There is no likelihood of that happening." Her face sobered, and for a moment he thought she would weep. "Be wary."

" 'Tis my true name, Wary O'Neill." He chuckled with his teasing.

She tilted her head. "Aye, your mother named you properly."

With those words, she moved across the field at a brisk pace. "You take heed," he whispered after her. Henry scrutinized the surroundings, ready to defend his beloved if necessary. One day they would have a delightful life together. He smiled at his word choice.

≈

The windows were already shuttered, barring Delight any view of the goings-on inside her home. Although she wanted to believe nothing was amiss, caution guided her steps. A peculiar sensation played with her mind, as though danger lurked about. She shrugged away the feeling, attributing it to her recent fever.

I promised Papa I would avoid dangerous situations, but dire straits seem to follow me wherever I go. As Papa protected me from Grace years ago, my heavenly Father will protect me and my loved ones now.

Every step became a prayer. She hesitated, listening intently for God's voice warning her to return to Henry; but she heard nothing, only felt the eerie chill at her nape.

Delight lifted the latch and slipped inside the front door as Henry had instructed. She heard the low hum of voices, not the expected laughter from her sisters. Normally Mercy and Hope would be playing. Of course they could be reading Scripture or praying or practicing their letters. Or the uneasiness racing through her might mean something truly frightening.

From the darkness a hand seized her upper arm. "You must

be the one we've been waiting for."

She gasped and struggled to free herself. "Sir, let me go!"

"Not until you answer a few questions." He gripped her tightly and squeezed, but she refused to cry out. "I believe we have our prize," he called out. Intensifying his hold, he pulled her toward the kitchen and a crackling fire.

At the sight of her mother's anguish-ridden face and the protective way she cradled Elijah, Delight experienced a mixture of anger and compassion unlike anything she'd ever known. "Mama." The word fell from her lips without thought.

"There is no need to treat her cruelly," Mama said, rising to her feet and cradling baby Elijah in her arms. Her carriage would have rivaled that of the king.

The soldier holding Delight, a pasty-looking fellow, sneered at her mother and intensified his hold. "I will consider letting her go when she responds properly to my questions."

Delight winced. "I am fine, Mama. Do not worry." She quickly glanced about the room. One other soldier and two men sat about the room. Their muskets and bayonets lay within easy reach, stacking the odds against Henry. Her sisters huddled together, frightened and pale, while indignation soared through Delight. But Charity, where was she?

Her gaze flew to a corner. James was propped against a wall with Charity beside him. In the next breath, she saw he'd been gagged. No doubt, he had been quite verbal.

"We're looking for Henry O'Neill," the pasty soldier spat out. "The deserter has our gunpowder."

"And you think I know where he is?"

"Your kind neighbor, Mistress Rutherford, said you left with him. Lass, do your family and your country a valued service and tell us where to find him."

That insufferable woman! To think I once sat beside her at the meetinghouse, believing she could be won over with Christian kindness. Delight stiffened. "If I did know his whereabouts, I would not tell the likes of you." For a moment, she thought the soldier would strike her.

"There is a reward, you know," another soldier reasoned.

Fury burned across her heart. "I have no need of your money."

The soldier who appeared to be in charge pushed her toward her mother. "Then wait with the others. He will return; we're sure of it. He'd not leave a lass as pretty as you without a farewell."

She caught her balance and seated herself by Remember and Faith. Patience looked to be on the verge of fainting. Delight offered a reassuring smile to her sisters before replying to the soldier. "He is most certainly miles from here by now."

"We will soon know for sure," the soldier replied. "I've been enjoying the fair lasses of this household; no wonder O'Neill sought to ignore his duty."

Disgusting pig! Don't you dare touch one of my sisters. Oh, God, forgive me. I know that Thy presence is here—and that Thou art in control. I am trusting Thee in this. Please tell me how to proceed.

A man shifted nearby to stare at her. He smelled of dirt and sweat, and his malevolent smile sickened her. As he rubbed the side of his jaw, she saw it: the brand of a thief.

The wicked men who had tried to kill James had found him again. Not only did revenge rule their motives, but also the deserter's fee from the British. God help them all against their enemies.

She peered at Charity and James. From what she could see, he looked considerably better than at their parting, and Charity appeared well. What ideas were rumbling through their heads?

Several long minutes passed. A plan began to emerge from Delight's frenzied mind. She prayed it came from God and not from her driving passion to take care of her loved ones.

"This is all your doing," she shouted at Charity.

Her sister blinked, obviously confused. *Please, Charity, this is a game. Henry will not stay away from the house forever. He will sense the trouble within and try to help.*

Hopefully, he can hear my voice and be alerted to what awaits him inside.

"Do you have nothing to say for yourself?" Delight flung at her sister.

"Whatever do you mean?" Charity stiffened.

"Hush," Mama said. "You will wake the baby."

"The baby is not my concern." Delight hoped her insincere remark—a long measure from her deep love for the wee babe—revealed her intentions. "She," and she pointed to the figure snuggled next to James, "played me for a fool."

"This is not the time to discuss such matters," Mama said, flashing her a bewildered look.

"I demand quiet," the soldier who had pained Delight ordered. His brow wrinkled in annoyance.

"Oh, you do?" She peered into the face of the disgusting, pasty-faced soldier. "None of us would be here against our will if not for my shameless sister."

One of the other redcoats chuckled. Well, he would surely be entertained this evening.

"You are merely angry because I outwitted you," Charity said, louder than Delight had ever heard her sister speak.

Her sister's twist encouraged Delight. "I took you at your word! Why are you there with James after all you've done?"

Charity lifted her nose and linked her arm with James's. "He is hurt, and I am making certain he is nursed properly."

"Nursed? Like you did poor Henry, filling him full of lies about your affections for him?"

" 'Tis not Henry's fault he found me more desirable than you."

I love you, Sister. Help me continue this charade.

"Enough," the lead soldier said, "or I will gag the both of you."

"How dare you threaten me?" Delight attempted to stand, but Patience and Faith held to her arms. Remember clasped her hands together, no doubt in prayer for the scene unfolding before her.

"Calm yourself. You can deal with Charity's fickle behavior later," Patience said, overcoming her innate shyness. "You should not be surprised by Charity since she vexes us all."

Good girl. If we stall for time and deter the soldiers' attention, Henry may be able to overtake them.

"Leave Charity alone," Faith insisted. "If you were fool enough to believe Henry preferred you to her, then so be it. You are simply jealous."

If not for the danger besetting them, Delight would have burst into laughter at the preposterous conversation. She took a quick breath and glanced at Mama. In the firelight, she had paled. Poor Mama, but the sisters were on a mission and Delight could explain later. "Envious. I dare say not. She has no conscience or loyalties."

Charity laughed. Elijah woke with a howl.

"See what your quarreling has done." Mama shifted the baby to her shoulder and patted his back.

"Henry simply wanted a diversion during his days of recovering." Charity smirked. Even in the shadows, her facial expressions conveyed the manner of a haughty young woman. "You amused and bored him, but I held his attention. Now he is gone and made quite the twit of you."

Patience raised her fist. "Have you no decency? He broke Delight's heart. And what of James? Did you not steal his affections, too?"

Mercy and Hope began to sob as Elijah broke into an ear-piercing scream.

Patience, you are a jewel. And Charity, I forgive all of your teasing from these past weeks. "Have you cast your charms upon these men as well?" Delight detected a movement in the shadows from where she'd entered the house. She must act hastily.

"Delight, you will stop at nothing," Charity sneered. "I feel sorry for you, yet intelligence never was your strength."

Delight shook off Faith and Patience's hold, scurried to her feet, and raced across the room toward her sister. She masked her fear with an incensed look, as though led by blind rage. Holding the captors' attention became foremost in her mind. The pasty-faced soldier seized her arm, and she pretended to stumble, knocking the musket from his hands and sending it crashing to the floor.

"That's about enough, chaps," Henry called from the doorway.

The other men reached for their weapons, but a second voice emerged from the shadows. "I would not be too hasty to put your hands on those guns," Uncle Matthew warned.

The one soldier still held on to Delight, but she used her foot to maneuver the musket in Charity's direction. Her sister snatched it up. "Let go of my sister, or I will spill your blood over that fancy red jacket."

Charity, from whence did such gumption arise?

The soldier's hand rose to Delight's throat. An icy sensation awakened fresh fear in her. "The hole will have to go through her first."

Panic creased Charity's face. Their game was over. Before Delight could struggle against her captor, Henry strode across the room and laid a fist into the soldier's jaw, forcing him to release her. Another punch left the man sprawling on the floor.

"Did he hurt ye?" Henry asked Delight, holding down the belligerent soldier.

Delight shook her head and demanded her trembling body to cease quaking.

Henry bent to tie the soldier's hands behind his back. "I should not have sent you inside without me," he murmured to Delight.

"We did not have any idea what had happened," she managed to say through a ragged breath. "I trusted God, and He did not fail us."

She saw the soft glow of love emitting from his eyes before he reverted his attention to the soldier and the men Uncle Matthew held at gunpoint. Suddenly it occurred to her that her uncle had jeopardized his life and his home by helping Henry.

"Uncle Matthew, what will you do after this?" Delight asked.

"I'm enlisting with Henry," he boasted. He looked so much like Papa. "Rather than hide from the redcoats, I plan to defend my country."

"You will meet your death," the branded thief said.

"Rather a noble grave than live under the tyranny of the king," Uncle Matthew replied. "You think about those things while you are in chains."

Charity quickly untied the knots binding James's mouth, then whirled and fell into Delight's arms. "I was so frightened for you."

"You were magnificent." Delight twirled her sister around the kitchen. "And so are our sisters. More so, our diversion worked."

In that instant, Elijah quieted while Mercy and Hope clung to their mother's skirts.

Charity smiled weakly before turning back to James.

"Remind me to never make the Butler women angry," he said. "I would not survive. What I just witnessed would shake any man's resolve." He clasped Charity's hand in his. "And you are full of surprises."

"I believe she had a good teacher," Henry said, urging the soldier to his feet. "In truth, my Delight is the epitome of a woman in love with her God, her country—"

"And her soon-to-be husband," Delight finished.

twenty-one

Delight shivered as she wriggled into her Sunday dress of indigo and white lace. Although the room had a distinct chill, she knew her shaking was due to anticipation of the wedding ceremony about to proceed. Nervous and excited best described her—and filled with a mountain of love for Henry.

Had it been only yesterday morning when she had fretted about her disobedience to God and her feelings for Henry? So much had occurred since then, and she had had so little time with him before he left with Uncle Matthew and James with the captured men. She prayed for an uneventful journey. Life certainly looked less perilous when she trusted God completely. Perhaps this way of thinking was what Papa meant all along. Not trusting God held more danger than anything man could conjure.

She wished he could be here this day to see her wed Henry, but he'd already given his blessing. When Papa received the news, he'd be pleased, and he'd have plenty of other weddings to attend once the war ended.

The war. She refused to let that reality darken her day. She must trust God, not simply today, but on every day of her life.

"Delight, are you ready?" Charity asked from the doorway. "Mama started to come, but then Elijah demanded to be fed."

"Almost. Would you straighten my hair? It has a willful mind today."

Charity picked up a brush and in a few quick strokes had Delight's locks secured into a bouquet of loops and curls.

"Perfect." Delight turned to give her sister a hug.

"I am so happy for you," Charity whispered through a sprinkling of tears.

"Oh, you are not rid of me. I will be around for awhile to

make your life interesting."

Her sister giggled. "Henry's life will never be boring."

"Oh, but I love him so much."

"And he loves you."

"Thank you for everything you have done," Delight whispered. "I will never forget your goodness."

"We shall see. I imagine I can think of several things to tease you about once Henry leaves in the morning."

A few moments later, Delight stood by Henry's side, his hand firmly clasped around hers. Devotion flowed from his fingertips to her heart and back again. She felt his gaze upon her, and she smiled into those blue pools of tenderness. Never had she been so certain of the life before her. The uncertainties of the days ahead lessened in her understanding of God's provision, the dreams of this wondrous country, and her love for Henry, her beloved turncoat.

A Letter To Our Readers

Dear Reader:

In order that we might better contribute to your reading enjoyment, we would appreciate your taking a few minutes to respond to the following questions. We welcome your comments and read each form and letter we receive. When completed, please return to the following:

Fiction Editor
Heartsong Presents
PO Box 719
Uhrichsville, Ohio 44683

1. Did you enjoy reading *The Turncoat* by DiAnn Mills?
   ❑ Very much! I would like to see more books by this author!
   ❑ Moderately. I would have enjoyed it more if

   _____
   _____
   _____

2. Are you a member of **Heartsong Presents**? ❑ Yes ❑ No
   If no, where did you purchase this book? _____
   _____

3. How would you rate, on a scale from 1 (poor) to 5 (superior), the cover design? _____

4. On a scale from 1 (poor) to 10 (superior), please rate the following elements.

   ____ Heroine   ____ Plot
   ____ Hero   ____ Inspirational theme
   ____ Setting   ____ Secondary characters

6. How has this book inspired your life?_____

_____

_____

7. What settings would you like to see covered in future
   Heartsong Presents books? _____

_____

_____

8. What are some inspirational themes you would like to see
   treated in future books? _____

_____

_____

9. Would you be interested in reading other **Heartsong
   Presents** titles? ❑ Yes ❑ No

10. Please check your age range:
     ❑ Under 18   ❑ 18-24
     ❑ 25-34   ❑ 35-45
     ❑ 46-55   ❑ Over 55

Name_____

Occupation _____

Address _____

City_____ State_____ Zip_____

E-mail_____

Presents

Great Inspirational Romance at a Great Price!

Heartsong Presents books are inspirational romances in contemporary and historical settings, designed to give you an enjoyable, spirit-lifting reading experience. You can choose wonderfully written titles from some of today's best authors like Peggy Darty, Sally Laity, Tracie Peterson, Colleen L. Reece, Debra White Smith, and many others.

When ordering quantities less than twelve, above titles are $3.25 each.
Not all titles may be available at time of order.

$\mathcal{H}$EARTSONG ♥ PRESENTS

Love Stories Are Rated G!

That's for godly, gratifying, and of course, great! If you love a thrilling love story but don't appreciate the sordidness of some popular paperback romances, **Heartsong Presents** is for you. In fact, **Heartsong Presents** is the only inspirational romance book club featuring love stories where Christian faith is the primary ingredient in a marriage relationship.

Sign up today to receive your first set of four, never-before-published Christian romances. Send no money now; you will receive a bill with the first shipment. You may cancel at any time without obligation, and if you aren't completely satisfied with any selection, you may return the books for an immediate refund!

Imagine. . .four new romances every four weeks—two historical, two contemporary—with men and women like you who long to meet the one God has chosen as the love of their lives. . .all for the low price of $10.99 postpaid.

To join, simply complete the coupon below and mail to the address provided. **Heartsong Presents** romances are rated G for another reason: They'll arrive Godspeed!

YES! Sign me up for Hearts♥ng!